V,L

"I don't follow dire

"How's that working for you, soldier?"

"At the moment?" Finn's hands settled lightly on Tucker's hips. "Jury's still out."

She refused to take a step back.

He liked that confidence. It was sexy as hell.

Finn flashed a wicked grin and bent his head, his mouth settling over hers, a warm demand. But instead of quenching the thirst he'd been fighting since he met her, that one taste only made him crave more. Damn, this wasn't smart. He was supposed to be finding a drug dealer, not kissing the hell out of a potential suspect.

Pulling back, he stared into her dazed eyes, unable to fight the curl of satisfaction that rolled through his belly. He'd done that to her. With one kiss. One mind-blowing kiss.

Tucker yanked out of Finn's arms and a bolt of anger flashed through her eyes as her palm connected with his cheek. The crack of skin on skin echoed through the empty bar...

Dear Reader,

I've loved every minute of writing my Military K-9 series. Not only was the research fun—can you say adorable dog videos?—but I've learned so much. The stories of bravery and sacrifice have tugged at my heartstrings over and over again.

For Finn McAllister, working with dogs was a side benefit to his real calling—getting drugs off the street. The tragic loss of his sister sent his life on a trajectory he hadn't quite expected, but he's still grateful for every day. On the other hand, Tucker Blackburn has been afraid of dogs since she was six. And she isn't happy at all when Finn and Duchess stroll into her bar. What starts out as a clash of wills soon ends with both of them discovering more than they expected about themselves and each other.

Military Working Dogs dedicate their lives to serving our country just like every other US soldier. But once they no longer serve a purpose, their journey back to a normal existence and a family who can love and support them is often difficult. However, there are organizations that provide funds and programs to assist in this transition. If you're interested in learning more, please visit missionk9rescue.org.

I hope you enjoy reading Finn, Tucker and Duchess's story! I'd love to hear from you at kirasinclair.com, or come chat with me on Twitter, @KiraSinclair.

Best wishes,

Kira

Kira Sinclair

Rescue Me

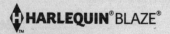

Recycling programs
for this product may
not exist in your area.

ISBN-13: 978-0-373-79925-1

Rescue Me

Copyright © 2016 by Kira Bazzel

Printed in U.S.A.

www.Harlequin.com

Kira Sinclair writes emotional, passionate contemporary romances. A double winner of the National Readers' Choice Award, her first foray into writing fiction was for a high school English assignment. Nothing could dampen her enthusiasm...not even being forced to read the love story aloud to the class. Writing about sexy heroes and strong women has always excited her. She lives with her two beautiful daughters in North Alabama. Kira loves to hear from readers at kirasinclair.com.

Books by Kira Sinclair

Harlequin Blaze

The Risk-Taker
She's No Angel
The Devil She Knows
Captivate Me
Testing the Limits
Bring Me to Life
Handle Me

SEALs of Fortune

Under the Surface
In Too Deep
Under Pressure

Island Nights

Bring It On
Take It Down
Rub It In

To get the inside scoop on Harlequin Blaze and its talented writers, visit Facebook.com/BlazeAuthors.

All backlist available in ebook format.

Visit the Author Profile page
at Harlequin.com for more titles.

For the dogs that have graced my life, shown me unconditional love and given true companionship— Bridget, Tippy, Ming, Jack and Emma. Gone, but never forgotten.

1

THE KENTUCKY ROSE looked like a good time.

Or what he was supposed to think was a good time. But that wasn't what had brought Finn McAllister out to the popular honky-tonk on a Friday night.

He could still see the drawn face of Sergeant Freeman lying in that hospital bed. The pallor of his skin as he'd explained where he'd bought the drugs that had landed him in the ER. From a woman at this bar.

The man had a long road ahead of him. Not just dealing with the physical aftermath of ODing and the legal consequences that would come with it, but the emotional issues that had the airman turning to illegal drugs for relief in the first place. It was a story Finn had seen all too often over the years.

In this instance, Freeman had been lucky. Three other airmen and a handful of civilians had lost their lives.

You'd think, after years of seeing the toll drugs could take on a person, Finn would have gotten used to it. That would never happen. Each time felt personal.

Maybe because each time reminded him too much of his sister, Bethany.

So tonight he was at the Kentucky Rose, hoping to find something that would help him shut down the pipeline of meth being funneled straight to the soldiers it was his job to protect.

The bar was fairly new, only open a little over a year. But according to the guys he'd talked to on base, it had generated a lot of buzz.

Gravel crunched beneath the heels of his boots. Not the hand-tooled leather boots he'd likely find inside, but the well-worn combat boots that had served him well most of his career. Broken in and comfortable.

Someone opened the door, and loud music spilled out into the night. Beside him, quiet as a shadow, Duchess, the military working dog he'd been handling for almost eight years, pricked her ears and scanned her surroundings.

Finn didn't go anywhere without Duchess, but tonight she was more than just along for the ride. Trained to scent drugs, she had a job to do. Just like he did.

"Let's get this over with," Finn murmured, giving her the signal to heel.

The mingled scents of beer, women and something earthy hit him as he walked through the heavy front door. The bar was huge, a big old wooden structure on the outskirts of San Antonio that, from the outside, looked like a run-down barn. But the inside...

The place was packed, even early on a Friday night. And not just with the wild boys from Lackland Air Force Base down the road. Men and women of all ages were mixing together. Laughing, dancing, sharing drinks.

"Hey, sugar. Can I get you anything?"

The redhead stared up at him with vibrant green

eyes. If she was a day over twenty-one then he'd eat Duchess's harness for breakfast tomorrow. Dewy, Southern-girl innocence clung to her like the scent of roses that swirled around him when she moved close.

Finn took the barest step away.

"A table and the darkest beer you have on draft."

The redhead twittered, countering his move by inching closer and settling a hand on his arm. *Dammit.* He really wasn't in the mood to get hit on by his waitress tonight. What he wanted was a dark, out-of-the-way corner, so he could sit and watch.

"The beer I can handle, but the table might be a problem. You should have gotten here a half hour ago if you wanted someplace to sit."

Shifting, Finn moved so that the waitress's hand fell away. "I'll remember that for next time."

"You do that," she said, flashing a megawatt smile that probably won her a lot of tips. He didn't have the heart to tell her it wouldn't get her anywhere with him.

Heading toward the back wall, Finn found an empty spot in the shadows. It would work. A good place to observe.

Off to the side, a rowdy group crowded around a mechanical bull. They let out a raucous cheer as a huge dude got bucked off, hitting the mats with a resounding thud.

On the other side of the bar, the dance floor was packed. Couples were bumping and grinding to the country music blaring from speakers strategically placed all around. And was that…? Yes, it was. The mirrored ball revolving lazily over the floor was shaped like an armadillo.

That pretty much summed up the place. Quintessentially Southern honky-tonk tacky.

Reaching behind him, Finn found Duchess's head and gave her a good scratch behind the ears. A German shepherd, Duchess was one of the best dogs he'd ever had the pleasure of handling.

Her demeanor was so calm, especially when working. Even as a puppy, she hadn't been rambunctious like the others in her litter. She could scent the smallest amount of marijuana, the tiniest packet of cocaine lodged in some of the most insane cavities on the human body. She was a machine, and a very well-behaved one.

Several feet away, a group of rowdy thirtysomethings began to gather their things from a table. Finn took several steps in that direction, intending to claim the space while he had the chance. He'd been on his feet since before dawn this morning, called by his commanding officer when word of Freeman's OD came in. His entire body ached, something he was hoping a beer would fix.

From the other direction, Finn noticed a group of college kids eyeing the same table. *Not on your life.*

Picking up the pace, Finn was intent on reaching it first, but a warm, golden voice had him halting in his tracks.

"What the hell do you think you're doing?"

It didn't help that the words were accompanied by the most compact little dynamo slipping right in front of him and blocking his path.

Her hands were balled on lush hips, blond hair cascading in curls down her back. The deepest blue eyes he'd ever seen flashed at him, full of outright anger.

Over her shoulder, Finn watched the competition

grab the chairs around the table, pull them out and plop their infantile butts down.

This was the most irritating end to a day full of shitty experiences.

"Hey, I'm talking to you. What the hell do you think you're doing?"

The tiny blonde, who tried to compensate for her five-foot-nothing height by wearing the most insanely impractical heels he'd ever seen in his life—even though she was still over half a foot shorter than he was— crowded into his personal space. Her finger landed in the center of his chest and she poked.

Her gaze darted behind him, landing on Duchess. Fear flashed across her expression before she tamped it down.

Great. It didn't happen often, but occasionally Finn encountered people who were afraid of dogs. And while Duchess was one of the sweetest, gentlest animals he'd ever met, there was no getting around the fact that she was big and could be intimidating. That impression wasn't helped when people learned she was a trained military dog.

Yes, she could take down bad guys, but only on command. Not that this woman wanted to hear that right now.

"You can't bring a dog into a bar. Get him out of here."

Finn cocked his head and for several seconds seriously considered picking her up and moving her out of his way. He bench-pressed more than she had to weigh. "Her."

"What?"

"My dog is a her. Just because she's big doesn't mean she's male."

Shaking her head, the sprite of a woman said, "She can be male, female or in the process of gender re-assignment for all I care. She doesn't belong in my bar. Get her out of here."

Her bar?

Finn let his gaze travel down her body again, a little more intrigued this time.

It fit. The impractical shoes were a perfect complement to the armadillo spinning lazily overhead. Her jeans were well worn and molded to her body. She might be small, but it was obvious she had curves in all the right places. And the black T-shirt she wore, emblazoned with the logo of a local craft beer, emphasized that fact.

As she leaned closer, the pressure from her finger increased. That was really beginning to irritate him.

"You have to leave," she reiterated.

He could argue with her—actually, Duchess was legally allowed to be on the premises. But considering his purpose for being at the Kentucky Rose in the first place, it probably wasn't a smart idea to piss off the owner. Yet.

So he'd try to cajole.

"I just ordered a beer."

"Too bad. Your dog isn't welcome."

Or maybe not.

Crossing his arms over his chest, Finn stared down at her. "My dog is a highly trained military working dog. She's a decorated war hero. She's a hell of a lot better behaved than half the people in this tacky excuse for a bar."

The minute the words were out of his mouth, Finn

realized he'd made a tactical error. She might have been angry before, but now she was downright pissed.

Her skin flushed a deep pink. Her eyes turned glacier, but somehow still had the ability to burn straight through his skin.

"Tucker." Someone yelled the name out across the crowd. He didn't realize the voice was addressing the woman in front of him until the brute attached to it appeared behind her. You could've fit her inside the man's clothes twice and had room to spare. But the guy was all frickin' muscle.

Not that it particularly mattered to Finn. He'd fought guys bigger and badder than this one and come out on top.

"You need help with this guy, Tucker?" he asked, keeping his gaze trained on Finn.

Tucker. That was interesting. He'd never have pegged her for a Tucker, although something about the name fit. Unusual and dynamic, just like the woman.

"Nope. He and his dog were just leaving." Her eyes flashed a warning. For some strange reason, he really wanted to ignore it, just to see what she'd do.

But out of the corner of his eye he saw several more men who were obviously the brute's backup slide into place on either side of him. Finn's mother hadn't raised a complete idiot.

"All right." Finn held up his hands. "Duchess and I will go." For now.

But they'd both be back. Because the Kentucky Rose was the first real lead in finding and stopping the meth that had cost them several soldiers in the last two months.

He wasn't about to walk away from that.

BLOWING A BREATH that fluttered her bangs over her eyes, Tucker watched the door slam shut behind the soldier and his dog.

It was a shame he'd been such an arrogant asshole— bringing a dog into a bar—because he was a gorgeous one.

She didn't mean to study the way his jeans clung to his tight ass as he'd walked away. Or the bulge of his strong biceps beneath the tight edge of his T-shirt. Or the sexy stubble that covered his cheeks and did nothing to hide the dimple in the center of his chin.

There was no question, the man was rough around the edges. She hadn't needed him to tell her he was military, she'd known it before he opened his mouth by the way he held himself. That alert, prepared-for-anything way his gaze had moved around the room.

She'd grown up with an airman, her dad the only real family she'd ever had. And while she loved him, she also knew damn well she wanted nothing to do with any more soldiers. She'd had her fill of the uncertainty and fear that came with living that life.

Which possibly made opening a bar right outside an Air Force base a little like selling water on the edge of the desert. A smart business decision, but terrible for her personal life, considering the majority of the men she met were ones she refused to consider dating.

Maybe she should've opened the Rose somewhere else, but San Antonio was familiar...comfortable. It was the first place in her entire life that had felt like home. She loved the Texas twang in everyone's voices. The Southern charm of the people who inhabited the city. The green landscape against the wide open skies. Hell, she even liked the humidity in the summer.

She'd spent enough of her life moving from one base to another, never really feeling like anywhere was home. Or being left behind while her only living parent was in the middle of a war zone. Growing up with that stress and uncertainty…nope, not interested in courting more.

The Kentucky Rose was her chance to finally grow some roots, have a place all her own that no one could ever take away from her.

Turning on her heel, Tucker took a second to let her gaze travel across her bar. Taking in the happy patrons and hardworking staff, a sense of pride and satisfaction filled her. This was what was important.

She'd done this. *Built* this all by herself with hard work and sheer grit.

There was one rowdy group of guys, apparently in town celebrating a bachelor party. They'd been slamming back shots since they walked in the door. She'd have to tell Matt to stay close in case they got stupid drunk and made trouble. She also made a mental note to send Kayla over with some nachos on the house. Hopefully, the food would soak up the alcohol and slow them down a bit.

The first strains of *The Devil Went Down to Georgia* pumped into the room. From every corner, waitresses started whooping. The patrons, especially the regulars who knew what was coming, joined in. As one, the girls moved toward the bar, jumping up onto the wooden surface Tucker had spent hours sanding herself. In perfect unison, her team began to kick and stomp to the music, following the choreography they'd spent hours learning.

Tucker's eagle eye watched each of them, looking for any small imperfection they could work on the next time they practiced. Her team often left those sessions dripping with sweat and groaning about how much of a taskmaster she could be. But they looked forward to them anyway. She made sure they still had fun, with lots of laughter and camaraderie.

This might be work, but she regarded every woman on her staff as a friend. Over the last year, she'd made a point to foster the idea that they were family, not just coworkers. And she really believed that. On the floor, it was important to look out for each other, especially during busy nights like tonight.

"Tucker." Wyatt walked up, his large shoulder brushing against hers. He'd been with her from the very beginning as her head of security. But they'd known each other longer than that. Wyatt had worked at the bar she'd managed while putting herself through grad school.

At one point he'd tried to get into her pants, but she'd shut him down damn fast. Almost as bad as messing with a military man would be sleeping with one of her coworkers or employees. She didn't mix business and pleasure.

Now they were just good friends. Wyatt often stayed late to walk her out. He'd become the overly protective little brother she'd never had. And since he and Michelle, one of her best waitresses, had been together for almost six months now, everything had worked out for the best anyway.

"Thanks for helping me handle that guy and his dog before."

"Didn't look like you needed much help, boss. As usual. You had things well in hand."

"Yeah, but it's always better to have backup. At least he was smart enough to realize he was outnumbered and should leave quietly. I would've hated to make a scene."

"But you would've done it anyway."

She shrugged. "Sure. If I needed to."

Wyatt nodded. They'd worked together long enough to know how the other operated.

"I see you sent Kayla over to defuse the bachelor nightmare that was brewing." Wyatt tipped his chin in the direction of the bar. The song had flipped over to something about a girl and a tractor. Her team had melted into the crowd, back at it, serving the customers.

Everyone except Kayla. She was sitting on the bar, her tiny shorts riding up and flashing the curve of her ass. She tossed her long mane of red curls and laughed, the throaty sound carrying across the bar.

One of the guys tried to run his hand up the outside of her thigh. Before he could get far, Kayla smacked his hand and let out another peal of laughter like it was a joke.

"Stay close to her," Tucker said, shaking her head.

A self-defense instructor and rape victim advocate by day, Kayla could take care of herself. But that didn't mean Tucker was willing to leave her without backup if she needed it.

"You got it, boss."

"And keep your eyes on your job, not on my dancer." She smacked his arm, offering a glare they both knew was fake because she couldn't quite keep her lips from twitching into a smile. Besides she didn't really mean it. He and Michelle were good for each other.

Wyatt tossed her a grin of his own and wandered closer to Kayla. She glanced up, gave him a little nod and half smile of appreciation before returning her attention to the guys crowding around her.

On a bright note, Kayla should get an amazing tip.

The money would definitely come in handy when she had to pay her tuition next semester. It wouldn't be long before she had her master's in psychology.

Tucker didn't suffer any fools. She only hired people who had intelligence and drive. Ambition was a prerequisite. She wanted her business to be a stepping stone to more for everyone who walked through the doors— just like it was quickly becoming the kernel of her own dream come to life.

Growing up, she didn't anticipate her calling in life would be to own a bar. But her entire outlook changed when she took a bartending gig at a little dive outside her college campus. At first, she was just looking for something that didn't require a lot of effort and brought home enough to pay her tuition.

But in no time, she'd fallen in love with the life, her coworkers and customers. There was something about the camaraderie that fed her soul just as much as the classes she crammed for each day. And when her aunt left her a decent inheritance, Tucker had decided to combine it with her newly minted MBA and open her own business.

Months of pouring over plans, market research, studying the industry to determine what she could offer that other bars couldn't…it hadn't been easy, but it was absolutely worth it. Almost a year later, she was well on her way to success.

Shoving away from the column she'd been leaning against, Tucker headed for the women's restroom to do a quick check. Pushing open the custom door made from reclaimed wood, she scooted past the line of waiting women with a smile and a murmured, "Excuse me."

Everyone seemed happy, which is what she always

liked to see. A couple of women were crowded around the long mirror, gossiping about a guy and reapplying gloss.

Grabbing a stack of heavy paper towels stamped with the Kentucky Rose logo, she refilled the first dispenser on the far side of the trough sink.

"Those napkin thingies are adorable," one of the women said. "That's what I love about this place. It's the little touches."

"Like the armadillo!" someone else exclaimed from behind the stall door.

"Thanks," Tucker said, flashing an appreciative smile. "This is my home and I want it to feel that way for everyone."

"Nicest bar I've ever been to," someone else said, before slipping out the door.

"Not pretentious or seedy. Welcoming."

That was exactly what she'd been going for with each and every detail she'd layered into her bar. Tucker turned to fill the dispenser at the opposite end of the counter, but stopped when something caught her eye. Someone had dropped trash along the back of the sinks.

It shouldn't bother her, but it did. She realized she ran a bar and that most people didn't treat it like their own place, but what kind of prick just left garbage on the counter when there was a can not three steps away?

Fishing between the wall and the towel tray, Tucker snagged a corner of whatever it was and tugged—but got a hell of a lot more than she'd expected.

It wasn't just some cellophane from a new tube of lip gloss or even a condom wrapper. There, in her hand, sat a small bag of white crystals.

Maybe she shouldn't have been surprised—again, it

was a bar, after all—but she was. Tucker had a strict rule and everyone who worked for her knew it. No drugs— using or selling—by staff or customers. Anyone suspected of being high was shown the door.

Tucker stared at the baggie in her hand. Small enough that none of the women around her even appeared to have noticed. What the hell was she supposed to do with it?

"Tucker? You in there?" Wyatt yelled through the partially opened door. "We've got a problem."

Crap. Tucker stuffed the bag into her pocket. One problem at a time.

2

FINN WAITED FOR about twenty minutes, watching the
people come and go from the shadows surrounding his
Jeep. Enough time that Tucker would assume he'd left,
hopefully get busy with something else and not notice
when he and Duchess slipped back inside.

He wasn't anywhere near finished with the Kentucky
Rose—or its feisty owner.

Waiting until a rowdy group of college guys crowded
the front door, he melded seamlessly with the group.
The guys pushed at each other, laughing and generally
making asses of themselves, never even noticing he was
amongst them. Idiots.

Blending into the shadows on the outskirts of the
room, Finn found a booth that was unoccupied—probably because it was far away from the dance floor, bull
and bar. Still, it worked perfectly for his purposes.

Duchess, her paws barely making a sound, curled
up beneath the sticky, gouged surface of the table. Her
head rested on his feet. To anyone who might spot her,
which was unlikely in this crowd, they'd probably think
she was napping. But Finn knew she was actually pay-

ing more attention to what was going on than half the people in the place.

He'd barely settled before a waitress swept over to his table. "What can I get you tonight?"

He ordered another beer. Maybe he'd actually get to drink this one. Several minutes later, the waitress plopped a frosty glass onto the table in front of him, apparently oblivious to the dog not three feet away.

Good. If he was lucky no one else would notice her, either.

Grasping the cold glass in his hand, Finn settled back into the corner of the booth, propping his legs up across the seat. The beer was good; he'd give Tucker that. A nice selection from a local microbrewery.

Finn watched, taking in the patrons and the staff. Looking for anything that stuck out to him as strange.

It didn't take long for Tucker to surface again. He watched her move efficiently through the crowd, stopping to encourage some women who were obviously out for a night without kids and husbands to indulge by taking a turn on the mechanical bull. They went from reluctant to whooping and hollering, huge smiles on their faces.

At another table, she nudged a group into purchasing more drinks. At the next, where an inebriated group of professionals had obviously overindulged, she pushed food and glasses of water, instead. She expertly maneuvered each of her customers into having a good time, and the most impressive part was, they had no idea it was happening.

But Finn noticed. Because paying attention was part of his job.

He tried not to let her distract him, but over and over

again he found his gaze drawn to her body, her smile, the way her face lit up when she laughed.

Several times he wished he had his camera so he could capture the flash of amusement as it stole through those bright blue eyes. Or the glint of light off those soft, golden curls. His fingers itched to hold the camera in his hands, to view her through the tiny window and see what else a photograph might expose about the woman he couldn't seem to ignore.

But leaving the camera tucked away behind the seat of his Jeep was the smart move. Having Duchess beside him was conspicuous enough; if he'd strolled in here with an expensive piece of equipment hanging around his neck, too…it would have been too much.

Finn finished his beer, flagged a passing waitress and requested another. He was fifteen or so minutes into the second when Tucker disappeared into the back. The crowd was getting rowdier, typical Friday night. The hand on his watch was creeping toward midnight. The mom crowd had headed home a while ago, to relieve their babysitters, leaving behind only the hard-core partiers and singles searching for a hookup.

The mix of professionals and college students was outnumbered by airmen. Even out of uniform, Finn had no trouble picking them out—both men and women looking for a good time.

Someone cranked the music just a little louder. Darkness draped over the dance floor like a curtain, only broken by the flash of laser lights bouncing off the walls and that damn mirrored armadillo hanging from the ceiling.

People were laughing, singing and dancing. To his left, someone started yelling, the sound loud enough to rise above the crowd. Finn was on his feet before he registered the intention. Duchess was right beside him, her shoulder even with his hip.

Twenty feet away, two large men were shouting at each other. Finn didn't have to guess; it was obvious to him they were both soldiers. Idiotic hotheads.

Chairs fell backward, clattering to the ground. Coming from opposite corners of the bar, three bouncers were headed for the melee, but it would take them too long to wade through the crush of people.

Finn was closer.

Gritting his teeth, he was halfway across the space when the first punch was thrown. The crunch of bone against bone echoed around him. Glass shattered on the wooden floor. One of the guys grunted, but Finn had no idea if it was the fool who'd thrown the punch or the idiot who'd taken it.

Unfortunately, it didn't stop there. Stunned, the punchee shook it off, then threw one of his own, landing a solid uppercut followed by a body shot. The other guy doubled over.

Another bruiser entered the fray, and then a fourth. Fantastic, just what he needed, these knuckleheads drawing attention to themselves and tearing up the place.

Finn was right there, but not fast enough to prevent this from turning into a true clusterfuck. The situation was deteriorating quickly as buddies, fueled by alcohol and big egos, backed up their buddies.

The situation was bad enough, but it got ten times worse when he saw the bright flash of blond hair ahead of him.

Shit. Where had she come from?

"Tucker, don't!" Finn hollered.

She glanced over her shoulder, saw him and frowned. But she also ignored him, turning away.

Goddammit.

She practically disappeared between the bruisers who were too busy slamming each other into the tables that had emptied around them to notice a woman shoving her way between them.

The first guy went to throw another punch, but Tucker stepped right in front. He was too drunk to react before his fist connected with her jaw.

Tucker's head snapped sideways. She swore, the low, throaty hum of the sound reverberating through Finn's chest and making his belly cramp. He watched, helpless, as her body crumpled to the ground.

Finn's heart thumped erratically behind his ribs. A sense of impending doom he hadn't experienced since coming home from Afghanistan overwhelmed him. They were going to trample her.

He found a burst of power, wading right between the flailing fists and brawling men, taking a couple of glancing blows across his ribs and shoulder that he didn't even feel. Reaching down, he gripped Tucker and hauled her up.

Wrapping his arms around her, he pushed his way back out of the melee, using his broad body to protect hers as much as possible.

As he passed one of the bouncers who had threatened to throw him out earlier, Finn growled, "Get a handle on this."

"Working on it. She okay?" the bouncer asked, nodding his head toward Tucker.

"Don't know." She wasn't fighting him, which was

a bad sign. What little he knew about the woman suggested she probably wasn't one to take kindly to being hauled about. Something he had to respect. But she also wasn't limp and lifeless, as he'd feared he might find her.

Confident the men Tucker had hired were capable of getting control now that they were close enough to the fight, Finn strode swiftly to the booth he'd been in minutes before. Duchess gave a low whimper, but was right behind him.

He eased Tucker down onto the vinyl seat, propping her against the wall before pulling back so he could look down at her.

He expected to find her a little dazed.

Instead, those dark blue eyes that always seemed to snag him raged with anger.

"What the hell do you think you're doing?"

Twice now she'd growled those words at him. He was really starting to hate that question. "Saving your ass, darlin'."

"My ass didn't need saving. It's perfectly capable of taking care of itself."

"Didn't look like it from where I was standing... looking down on you sprawled across the floor."

Pulling her feet back, she tried to jerk up and sit straight.

Finn grasped her calves and pinned her legs right where they were. "Oh, no, you don't."

"Get your hands off of me."

"Gladly, as soon as you promise to stay put."

"I have to handle the situation."

Finn threw a glance over his shoulder. Five bouncers had swarmed the area and were each manhandling a soldier in the general direction of the door.

"Your security team has it well in hand."

"I'm sure they do, but that doesn't mean I don't need to be there. This is my place. It's my responsibility."

His lips twitched. "I imagine you pay good money for men who can handle this kind of thing for you. Let them earn their paychecks. You had the wind knocked out of you."

He watched her little button nose scrunch up and her soft pink mouth twist into a grimace. A shudder ripped through her body and she finally sagged against the side of the booth. "God, I can't believe I didn't see that punch coming."

Bowing her head, she started to probe along her cheekbone. He didn't miss her wince. The skin was already starting to mottle. In a few hours she was going to have one hell of a bruise across her cheek.

"I'm damn impressed."

Her gaze flashed up to him before dropping back to the table again. "Yeah, my guys are good. I only hire the best."

"I wasn't talking about your staff. I was talking about how well you took that punch. He was one hulking dude and put everything he had behind that hit."

"My cheekbone is throbbing with the proof of that."

"I know some pretty badass women, and I don't think any of them could have taken that hit and still been coherent enough to hold a conversation with me right now. Why isn't your brain rattled?"

She shrugged. "Not the first punch I've ever taken."

Shit. For the second time tonight, Finn wanted to

knock someone on their ass—preferably anyone who'd ever given Tucker bruises.

She must have registered where his brain had gone because she quickly said, "No. Not that way." She scoffed, the rough sound scraping through her throat. "I've been involved in martial arts and self-defense off and on for years. I was raised by a single dad who believed in making sure his little girl could take care of herself."

"Smart man."

"He is. But that's all I meant by not the first time I've taken a punch."

Satisfied she was showing no signs of concussion, Finn turned away long enough to snag the arm of a passing waitress and request she bring him a towel or bag filled with ice.

He might not know her well, but even Finn realized it was a testament to just how much her cheek must be hurting that Tucker didn't make some snide comment about him ordering her staff around. Or that after the waitress returned with some ice wrapped in a towel, she didn't protest when Finn moved close, sliding his hip against hers, to place it against her cheek.

But she did hiss and jerk back in response to the pain and cold.

Finn wrapped a hand around the back of her neck, holding her in place.

"That hurts," she grumbled.

What was wrong with him? He wanted to pick her up, plop her down into his lap and do whatever it took to make the pain go away. Even though he knew that wasn't possible.

The only person Finn ever worried about taking care of was Duchess—and she wasn't technically a person.

"I'm sorry, but something tells me you'd rather keep the swelling and bruising to a minimum."

With a sigh, she settled against the wall, the warmth of his palm cupping her head. The soft rain of her hair brushed across the back of his hand.

His gaze snagged on her lips. He wanted to taste them. Wanted to know if the taste of her would be just as spicy as her attitude, or if that prickly outer shell hid a sweetness designed to bring a man to his knees.

But he didn't get the chance. He could feel the presence behind him long before the man spoke.

"Boss, problem's all taken care of."

"Great. Thanks, Wyatt."

"You okay?"

"She's good. Looks like she'll have one hell of a bruise tomorrow, though."

The toe of her shoe connected with his hip. "I can speak for myself, thank you very much." Her gaze shifted to the man standing just over his shoulder. "I'm fine. Give me a few minutes and I'll be back out on the floor."

"Take your time. The guys and I have everything in hand."

Finn watched Wyatt disappear. Beside him, Duchess stirred. She moved to follow and Finn was too preoccupied to notice or call her back. He wasn't worried about her—she was better behaved than the morons they'd just thrown out.

"Hey, how the hell did you get back in, anyway? I'm pretty sure I said you and your dog weren't welcome."

"And yet we weren't the ones who just tried to start a riot in the middle of your bar."

"That's a little melodramatic, don't you think?"

Finn shrugged. "I'm not the one sitting here with an ice pack on his cheek."

She shoved at him. Finn moved so Tucker could slide out of the booth. He figured asking her to sit still a little longer wouldn't have made any difference. He could have stonewalled and kept her in, but he wouldn't put it past her to duck under the table.

The minute she stood she let out a loud hiss and her entire body buckled again.

Jolting forward, Finn caught her around the waist, not bothering to wait before depositing her back onto the bench.

Kneeling in front of her, he asked, "What's hurting?" even as his gaze swept over her looking for apparent signs of injury.

"My ankle. I must have twisted it when I got knocked on my ass."

His mouth tugged into a frown. "It's no wonder with these death traps you seem to think are shoes."

Slipping one of the heels from her left foot, he dropped it onto the floor, not caring when it clattered with a resounding bang.

"Hey!" She jerked forward, trying to dive after the shiny black heel. "Those cost eight hundred dollars."

Finn wrapped his fingers around her ankle, the smooth warmth of her skin registering somewhere deep inside. "Excuse me?"

"They're couture."

"Did you just tell me that you spent almost as much

as my mortgage payment on an impractical pair of heels?"

For the briefest moment, Tucker looked a little sheepish. But the expression didn't last long, quickly replaced with bravado and a no-nonsense stare that threatened to cut straight through him.

God, there was something about this woman that lit up everything inside him. She was infuriating and adorable at the same time. Intriguing and tempting.

"I don't need to justify my spending habits to you."

"No, you sure don't," he said, tucking his chin into his chest to hide the smile he couldn't quite stop. Probing her ankle, he moved it from side to side, testing her range of motion. So far, it wasn't swelling, which was a good sign. "But maybe you should lay off the heels for a few days while this heals."

She harrumphed, crossing her arms over her chest, but didn't argue with him.

Slipping the other shoe off, this time carefully setting it onto the floor beside them, Finn grasped her by the arms and gently pulled her up, taking as much of her weight as she'd let him.

"Try putting some weight on it."

Gingerly, she did, only grimacing slightly, before shaking his hands away. "I'm fine."

His fingers tingled where they'd touched her skin.

Scooping her shoes up, she limped away.

Shaking his head, Finn debated whether to let her go or try to help. It was obvious which she wanted. But before he could make up his mind, a commotion snagged his attention.

Several feet away, Duchess was raising a ruckus, barking and pawing at the floor.

Finn stilled. There was only one thing that would cause the dog to react that way.

"What the hell?" Tucker flashed him a glare. "If she leaves so much as a scratch on my floor I'm sending you the repair bill."

"Darlin'," Finn said. "You've got a bigger problem than a scuffed floor. Duchess only reacts that way to one thing."

"I hardly think she's found an IED buried beneath the floorboards, soldier."

"No. Duchess isn't trained to scent bombs."

Pushing ahead of her, Finn stalked over to where Duchess was going crazy. A couple of tables had been pushed out of the way during the fight, and right there, tucked halfway beneath the leg of one of them was a plastic bag filled with a decent amount of crystal meth. Not the kind of baggie sold for a single hit of fun... this was a big enough score that it would be broken up and sold.

"Drugs. Duchess is trained to find drugs."

Sonofabitch. That's what she wanted to say, but she managed to not let the word out. Not because she particularly cared what the man standing beside her thought of her vocabulary—she'd been raised by a soldier and she owned a bar. Her dictionary of curse words was understandably intense. But giving in to that urge would probably lead to a serious meltdown that she didn't have the luxury of indulging in right now.

Tucker stared at the little baggie dangling from the soldier's fingers. Twice in one night. Her teeth ground together. Taking a deep breath, she dragged her gaze up.

"Well, that's a problem."

A big one. Finding that bag in the bathroom was one thing. Sure, she did what she could to keep drugs out of her bar, but it was inevitable that some might slip through.

But him finding a sizable amount on the floor, the same night, was more than a coincidence. It was a major issue, one she and Wyatt would have to address.

"Really?" His dry tone irritated the hell out of her.

She moved to take the bag, but he snatched it out of her reach, holding it above her. "No, you don't."

So frustrating. Tucker tipped her head back and glared at the drugs dangling above her.

"What? I wasn't planning on using it."

"Sure."

Crossing her arms over her chest, she scowled at him. "I try my damnedest to keep that shit out of my place, but I'm not naive enough to think it doesn't still get in."

"So you intend to turn this over to the police?"

"Why would I do that? It isn't like the drugs can be traced to a person. They were lying on the floor. I'll just…flush them down the toilet." That was exactly what she needed to do.

"Uh-uh."

"Look…" Tucker's voice trailed off and she realized that she didn't even know his freakin' name. He'd picked her up off the floor, sent her blood pressure spiking as his palm cupped the back of her head, held an ice pack to her throbbing cheek and she didn't even know his name.

Maybe she should keep it that way.

"Finn McAllister."

"And Duchess." She knew the dog's name. The dog she didn't like to even glance at because it sent a zing of apprehension through her chest. "Look, Finn, I appreci- ate you sticking your nose in where it doesn't belong."

"Gee, what an amazingly passive aggressive ex- pression of appreciation."

Tucker let out a sigh. "Fine. Thank you for stepping in and helping with our little problem. And for mak- ing sure I was okay." Even she heard the reluctance in her words.

"Wow," he said, a smile stretching across his gor- geous mouth. No man should have lips like that, per- fect and lush, the thin white scar running through the right edge only making him more dangerously tempt- ing. "That might have been even worse."

"No, I really mean it."

She did. While it grated that she'd needed the help, she was big enough to realize it was the truth. No doubt she'd get another lecture from Wyatt when this was all over. He was constantly telling her not to get in the middle of altercations and just let him and the guys do their jobs.

But she had a hard time taking a step back and watching anyone protect what she'd worked so hard to build.

Her father had raised her to be self-reliant and in- dependent. She could still hear his voice in her head, telling her she was a big girl and needed to be strong, right before he left her by herself for months. She hadn't disappointed him then and she had no intention of start- ing now.

Even if there were days she felt...alone.

Despite the sense of family she tried to build within her team, they came and went. As much as she hated it, she was used to a fluid train of people moving in and out of her life. Moving around a lot as a kid, she'd become adept at being friendly with everyone, but not actually forming friendships because it always tore her heart out when those bonds were inevitably broken.

She'd built those old, protective walls pretty strong and high. Now, she wasn't sure she knew how to find a door—or even a crack—to let someone in. Not really.

Her cheek throbbed, her ankle and ass hurt, and her head was starting to pound, from stress, the punch, whatever. She was done dealing with this mess.

And this man.

Taking a step away, she said, "I'm assuming since your dog is trained to scent drugs that you know the best way to destroy that." She nodded at the baggie still suspended above her head. "I'm going to trust you to take care of it, but if you decide to smoke it…"

"Not happening."

"Whatever. If you decide to use it yourself I don't want to hear about it if you OD."

The corners of his lips turned up slightly, not nearly a smile, but definitely humor at what she'd said. The idea that he was silently laughing at her burned.

Slowly, he lowered his hand. Arms crossed over his chest, feet spread wide like he was king of the castle surveying his domain, his gaze ran over her. In the middle of a crowded bar he suddenly made her feel like the only person present. How the hell did he do that?

"You know something?" he finally said. "You're cute."

Tucker gave a fake gasp. "I've never heard that in my entire life."

Between her small stature, long blond curls and re-fined facial features, people tended to take one look at

Rescue Me

her and see sweet and soft. There was a large part of her that delighted in proving those people wrong because she was neither of those things.

Finn, however, simply ignored her sarcasm. "And I wouldn't touch the stuff if someone was holding a gun to my head. I've seen the results firsthand. It's nasty."

Tucker could hear the bitterness in his words, but didn't want to care. She definitely didn't want to ask.

It didn't matter anyway. In the next five minutes he was going walk out of her bar and out of her life.

"I have a business to run and a nasty bruise to ice. I'd appreciate it if you and your dog left my premises."

"Nice way to repay us for the help."

She shrugged. "My bar, my decisions. The sign outside the front door clearly says I have the right to refuse service to anyone I choose. Your tab's on me. Have a good life, Finn McAllister."

3

SITTING ON THE balcony off his bedroom, Finn stared at the sun rising over the flat green landscape and into the wide-open sky. He'd spent years in other places, but San Antonio had always been home. His parents still lived in the suburb he'd grown up in not far away.

One of the main reasons he'd bought this house was for the unencumbered view. Sure, off in the distance he could see the high rises of the city, but here…he'd found some peace. Although, tonight it had done little to settle the jumble of nerves and emotions churning inside him.

His gaze snagged on the baggie of crystal meth that sat on the table in front of him. He'd placed it inside an evidence bag. Later in the morning he'd contact Officers Dade and Simmons, members of the joint task force he and Duchess had been assigned to assist, and turn it over. If they got lucky maybe they'd get some prints and another lead.

Eventually, they'd get back the chemical analysis, which could tie this batch to the others that had been discovered at the scenes of the deaths they were investigating.

The fine crystalline powder stared at him. Mocked him. But he couldn't look away.

God, he hated that drug. Hated all of them, really, but he hated meth with a fiery passion. He wasn't lying to Tucker when he said he'd seen the cost of the high it brought. Ultra addictive, it didn't discriminate in the lives it destroyed.

His sister had been beautiful, popular, intelligent. She'd been in the top of her class, well on her way to an academic scholarship at a good college. No one in her life would've imagined she'd become an addict and OD, dying just two months before her high school graduation.

Finn could still see the image of her pale, lifeless body on that cold metal slab in the morgue. He'd been the one to identify her, his parents both too devastated to do it.

That experience had changed the trajectory of his own life. He'd already been in the Air Force, headed to the K9 training unit. When they'd offered him the chance to train with a drug dog instead of a bomb dog he'd jumped at the offer, joining a new mission that specialized in combating the increasing use of illegal drugs among soldiers.

He'd do anything he could to get drugs off the streets and get soldiers proper help for the stress they were under.

Now though, he and Duchess were out of active duty. Transferred to the training center so he could ensure the next crop of K9 handlers had the skills they needed to perform their jobs.

"Duchess, heel."

The first soldier who'd ODed had been a tragedy.

Well, truly, all of them were. But when the third one died, Finn and Duchess, because of their experience and specialized skills, had been temporarily assigned to a team from the drug enforcement unit. The General himself had given Finn a clear directive saying that stopping the flow of meth onto the base was his top priority.

Finn already knew exactly what Dade and Simmons were going to say when he told them what had happened. It was clear someone needed to keep an eye on the Kentucky Rose, and he had every intention of volunteering for the job.

From what Freeman had told them, they were looking for a woman. Thanks to the drugs, the man's memory was weakened and he hadn't been able to give them much to go on. He recalled her long hair and the fact that she was shorter than he was, but the rest of the details were fuzzy. They were hoping a couple of days' rest would help him remember more.

Finn had Googled the fiery blond bar owner and he'd had to wonder, given that Tucker Blackburn fit the admittedly broad description they had, if she might be involved in some way. But either she was an award-worthy actress or her reaction to drugs in her bar was genuine. He'd watched the emotions flit across her face, unguarded and unchecked—bewilderment, irritation, anger and then disgust.

For the moment, he decided to operate under the belief she was unaware. Which, if it was true, only made him angrier. This was not going to be a picnic and there was a part of him that raged on her behalf for being dragged into this mess.

But there was nothing he could do about that. The Kentucky Rose was smack in the middle of it all, and if he had his way the inconvenience was going to get bigger before it got better. The best he could do was try to protect her.

Even if she wasn't going to like his methods.

THE NEXT AFTERNOON Tucker stood in the middle of the Rose and tipped her head back. Closing her eyes, she let the silence and scents of the place soak into her. This was her favorite time of day. Before they opened. Before any of the staff arrived. When it was just her and the place she'd built.

Some people didn't like bars when they were empty. With the lights glaring, you could pick out all the scars on the bar and the rough edges of the walls. The tables were stark instead of inviting. Pretty colors didn't twirl across the dance floor, beckoning you to take risks and try moves you possibly shouldn't.

Monique, one of her oldest friends, often said the place was a little creepy when it was empty. Too big and…bare.

Tucker liked it because it was all hers.

An ugly purple and yellow bruise had bloomed over her cheek, but she'd managed to cover up the worst of it with makeup. Not that she particularly cared. She just didn't want to deal with the questioning looks and raised eyebrows it seemed to cause.

Her ankle was a little more troublesome. She'd bought a thin bandage brace, which was helping, downed several ibuprofen and forsaken her fancy heels—she really missed those extra few inches—for a pair of brown and teal cowboy boots that offered a little more support.

She'd try and take it easy tonight. Last night had been long and crazy. It had felt like everything that could go wrong did, capped off with the realization that the drugs Finn had found were apparently the same ones she'd discovered in the bathroom. The bag must have fallen out of her pocket when she got knocked on her rear in the fight.

Which was both good and bad.

Maybe the problem wasn't as bad as Finn seemed to think. Either way, he'd taken the drugs and hopefully disposed of them as he'd said he would. At the moment her best option was to view the situation as one less thing on her to-do list. And, with any luck, tonight would be less insane. Although it was a Saturday, so she wasn't holding her breath.

For right now, she needed to get the place ready. Tucker walked behind the bar and began taking inventory of what she needed to replenish from the back stock room. They'd gone through a ton of whiskey and vodka last night. She also needed several cases of beer.

She was lost in her own world and the familiar minutia when a loud knock echoed through the place.

Tucker frowned. The last thing she wanted to deal with was some idiot who thought she should be open merely because he was ready to start drinking.

Grabbing the stun gun she kept tucked behind the bar, she headed for the front door.

It was made of old, solid wood she'd found at a flea market, and she'd commissioned a local artist to carve it into a door, adding the bar's logo to the scarred surface. She loved that door. It was one of the first things she'd had made when she decided to open the place.

The only downside was that she couldn't see who was waiting on the other side. And since it was possibly one of her staff instead of an idiot customer who couldn't read signs or tell time, she flipped the locks and pulled the door open several inches.

She should have let them pound away.

Standing on the other side, were two officers, their badges already out, ready to flash in her face. And behind them stood Finn McAllister, Duchess sitting prettily at his side.

"Hi, Tucker. Can we come in?"

She should have known he'd come back to haunt her.

"Considering your friends, I'm going to guess I don't have much choice in the way I answer that question."

"No, ma'am," one of the officers said, his voice apologetic. "I'm Officer Dade and this is my partner, Officer Simmons. We have a few questions for you."

With a sigh, Tucker swept the door open, gesturing them inside with the business end of her stun gun.

"Please put the weapon down, ma'am," Simmons said, his hand already sitting on the butt of his own gun.

"Don't worry. I'll put it away behind the bar. I might not be thrilled to see you standing at my front door, but I'm not about to shock you. A girl can't be too careful, though."

"No, ma'am."

Tucker turned and started walking through the bar, doing everything she could to hide her limp. For some reason, she didn't want Finn to know her ankle was still bothering her.

"Finn, make yourself useful and lock the door behind you, would you?"

One of the men snorted, but she wasn't sure which one and didn't particularly care to find out.

Slipping the stun gun back into its hiding place, she

spread her arms wide along the business side of the bar. "Can I offer you gentlemen a drink?"

"We're on the clock, but appreciate the offer." Dade declined with a subdued smile.

She hadn't expected them to accept, but she was wise enough to make the offer anyway. "Then let's skip straight to why you're here. I'm sure Mr. McAllister notified you his dog discovered some drugs here last night. It won't surprise you to hear that happens sometimes in this business, despite my best efforts to eliminate it. I don't condone drug use. And, unlike other bars, neither I nor my security team look the other way when it happens."

Officer Dade nodded his head. "That's good to hear. But this isn't simply a case of someone partying too much."

"I'm afraid I don't understand."

Officer Simmons chimed in. "The bag Duchess discovered contained enough crystal meth to qualify as possession with the intent to distribute."

A heavy pit opened up in her belly. "You're telling me this isn't just college kids looking to have a good time. Someone was dealing inside my bar."

It wasn't really a question, but Simmons answered anyway. "We think so, yes."

Crap, she really hadn't wanted to hear that. This was a bigger problem than she'd realized.

"We have reason to believe someone has been using the Kentucky Rose to distribute. Any thoughts on who might be doing that? Suspicious regulars? Anyone who's been hanging out over the last few months, giving you an uncomfortable vibe?"

Maybe they didn't need a drink, but she did. Scooting down the bar, Tucker grabbed a glass, scooped some ice then filled it with water. The cool liquid eased her suddenly dry throat, but did nothing to soothe the sick churning in her belly.

"No. As I pointed out to Finn last night, I have the right to refuse service to anyone. My guys are trained to spot troublemakers and we bounce them as soon as we identify a problem. Anyone who might've raised a red flag wouldn't have been hanging around for long."

Finn finally chimed in, "What about your staff?"

For the first time since they'd walked in, Tucker looked at him. And then regretted it. Which was why she'd been avoiding him in the first place.

The stubble covering his chiseled face, the divot right in the center of his chin she wanted to run her tongue over. The way his watchful green eyes skimmed across her face, eliciting a tempting hum of awareness… Yep, pure trouble.

Her body's reaction was irritating. And unsettling.

Which was probably why she barked out her answer when she really hadn't meant to. "None of my staff would be that stupid."

Finn quirked a single eyebrow, calling her statement into question with nothing more than the gesture.

That didn't help settle her. "They're loyal, Finn. We're tight. We look out for each other and they understand how important the Rose is to me. They'd never do anything to jeopardize my business."

"You hope," he muttered under his breath.

"I know," she said, her words ringing with finality. Because even the thought of someone close to her doing this hurt. It couldn't be her staff.

Tying the Rose to drugs and dealing could have disastrous consequences for her business. The last thing she needed was to headline the six o'clock news with a story about a drug bust at her bar. Contrary to popular belief, not all publicity was good publicity. That kind of story could sink the good reputation she'd built this place on. Marketing was everything in this business, setting her apart from the numerous other bars in the city. With so many options, one bad story would easily send her customers elsewhere.

Not to mention the potential for her to lose her business and liquor licenses.

"Gentlemen, are you sure you're not jumping to conclusions? The bar was busy last night, as it is most Fridays. We were wall-to-wall people by the time Duchess found the drugs. Not to mention there'd been a fight. I suppose they could have belonged to one of the guys involved, but of course, I can't say for certain. And I'm not willing to assign blame to someone just because they were acting like a drunken idiot."

Dade grunted. "Do you have security cameras?"

Crap. Something dark started squirming through her belly. There was no telling what they'd find on her security footage. She normally scanned through the tapes with Wyatt every couple weeks, but they hadn't had a chance lately. It was entirely possible they'd discover the drugs falling from *her* pocket in that fight.

There was no good way to explain that, at least not at this point. Anything she said would look like a lie to cover her own ass.

The only way she was turning over the security footage was if she viewed it first.

"Yes, I have cameras, but they don't cover the entire place," she hedged. "I record the parking lots, front and back, all entrances, including the one employees use. I have a couple strategically placed on high traffic areas and the back stock room, just in case of theft. But the bar is too big to have cameras covering every square inch, and there's also a little issue called privacy."

"Still, we might get lucky and find something useful."

Tucker tried to keep her posture and voice level. "I'll ask my head of security to pull the footage together for you. Might take a couple days. Weekends are our busiest time."

She tried not to squirm, but it was difficult beneath Finn's strong, steady gaze. She didn't like the way he was watching her.

Or maybe that was just her own guilty conscience projecting.

Finn shifted. "Listen, Tucker. This isn't just about a drug dealer. There's been a trend of deaths from people ODing on crystal meth over the past eight months. A joint task force has been formed to try and find the source of the drugs and shut it down."

Her eyes flitted to Duchess. "And you're involved."

"Duchess and I have some unique skills and we've been temporarily assigned to the team. We want to find these guys just as much as the police."

Tucker let her gaze swing between the three men leaning against her bar. The expressions on their faces made her belly dip. Dade stared hard at her, as if he could force her to do whatever he wanted by sheer force of will. Simmons's face was half cajoling and half apology.

Finn's expression was shuttered and unreadable.

Turning to face him, she asked, "What do you want?"

"An airman who was revived after ODing told me he purchased the drugs here. From a woman."

"Well that narrows it down." Realization hit her like a bolt of lightning. "That's why you and Duchess were here last night."

That pissed her off. Why the hell hadn't he come to her? Let her know what was going on and why he was there? She wouldn't have made a fuss about the dog then.

"Yes. This is the first break we've had in the case, Tucker. Months of frustrating searches that've led nowhere while more men and women die."

What was she supposed to say to that? No, she didn't like the idea of people dying. Yes, she wanted to help if she could.

"Again, what do you want?"

Finn leaned across her bar, putting himself closer and making her want to move in the opposite direction. But she didn't. She wouldn't give him the satisfaction of knowing he affected her.

"To put someone here undercover."

A buzz of energy crackled across Tucker's skin. "And I don't suppose Dade or Simmons have been tapped for that assignment."

"Nope," Finn shook his head. "Duchess and I have."

Of course. "I don't like dogs."

"You don't say…" His dry tone scraped down her spine.

"And just how do you expect to integrate with my team? Want me to hire you as a new bouncer? Everyone on staff knows I'm not looking."

"No. We were thinking a little more intimate…more access." Finn's eyes flashed, ripping down her body quickly before zeroing back in on her gaze. "You dating anyone, Tucker?"

That rollercoaster ride her tummy was on took a major free fall.

"No."

"You are now."

4

"I DON'T WANT you here."

"Yeah, you've made that abundantly clear."

Dade and Simmons had left. For the last thirty minutes Finn had been trying to calm Tucker down. It wasn't working very well. She was pissed, and he supposed he didn't really blame her.

Not that it would make much of a difference.

They couldn't force her to cooperate, but he'd already figured out she was going to go along with their plan. If she wasn't, she wouldn't be so upset. She'd have simply told him to leave. Or waited until some of her muscle showed up and had them throw him out. Or at least try.

Instead, she'd been raining down words over his head, calling into question his parentage and the size of his package, and insulting just about anything else she could think of. The woman had an inventive vocabulary. He'd give her that.

In fact, watching her go off on her tirade was rather entertaining, not that he'd admit that to her.

What he found most intriguing was that her ass-chewing didn't seem to slow her down one iota, her words punctuated by slamming cabinets and drawers, clanging glasses. He was impressed that she could continue a steady monologue while hauling what had to be a hundred pounds of bottles.

And God forbid he offer to carry them for her.

He'd realized very quickly that attempting to share the load just led to more tongue-lashing—and not the kind he actually wanted.

So he and Duchess had decided to take a seat at the bar and just watch.

Damn, she was gorgeous. What he wouldn't do to be able to capture the tiny whirlwind of activity on film, though he doubted his amateur skills could do her justice. She didn't let anything derail her—not the bum ankle she was trying to hide, his unexpected visit or the proposition he'd delivered.

Her skin flushed with exertion and anger. Her blonde curls were wild and begging to be tamed—like the rest of her.

Her prickly attitude made him want to grab her, swing her into his arms and give her something else to occupy her mouth besides the barrage of words. Something inside him wanted to soothe her, distract her, channel that energy.

For the first time since she'd started, Tucker stopped. Or rather, her body stopped while her mouth kept moving.

"Stop staring at me."

"I'm not."

Her hands landed on her hips, one cocking out to the side as she tossed that long mane of hair over her shoulder. Her bangs curled into her flashing blue eyes, but she didn't seem to notice. Or care.

"You are. Stop it."

He'd let her spill her anger because he was hoping the well would eventually run dry. Unfortunately, he was starting to think that wasn't going to happen.

Time to change tactics.

Standing up, he scooted around the end of the bar. Tucker shifted on her feet, but didn't retreat. Maybe she should have.

Her head tipped as he moved close, heat and awareness hitting her glare. Her expression sliced right through him, the combination of anger and passion stirring something deep inside him.

Was she this fiery and explosive in bed? Finn had no doubt. Like trying to grab hold of lightning. Dangerous and exhilarating.

"Sweetheart, you can't strut around in skin-tight jeans, a T-shirt that clings to every curve you own, and that wild mane of hair, and not expect some attention. Surely, you're used to it by now."

Tucker's soft pink mouth thinned. It was naturally that color and he much preferred it to the shiny pink gloss it had been painted with last night. Not that the image of her taking him into her slick mouth hadn't flashed through his thoughts more than once since then.

"No, actually, I'm not. I've worked in bars for most of my adult life. I know what men usually go for, and it isn't my boyish frame."

What the hell was she talking about? "The only thing about you that screams boy is your name. Trust me, the rest of you is all woman and I am not the only man who's noticed."

Closing the space between them, Finn gave in and cupped the back of her neck with his palm. Her body vibrated with her irritation, energy arcing across his skin where he touched. Soft curls cascaded over his fingers and he used his hold to tip her head back. God, a man could get lost inside her dark blue eyes. He'd never seen anything like them. Just like the rest of her, they were gorgeous. Unusual.

"I'm going to hazard a guess that the men give you a wide berth not because they're not interested, but because you have a *Do Not Touch* sign blazing above your forehead in bright letters."

Tucker scoffed, the sound scraping through her throat. "Yeah, right. Hasn't stopped you."

"I don't follow directions very well."

"So I've noticed."

So much about this woman intrigued him. She might be terribly tiny, but her attitude said she was ten feet tall and could tackle anything in front of her.

He liked that confidence. It was sexy as hell.

Keeping his hold light, Finn slowly began guiding Tucker backward. It was a dance, one they'd been skirting around since last night. Considering the job he had to do and the role he was taking on, maybe it was better to get this out of the way now. Diffuse the tension building unchecked between them. Especially since they were going to be playing the boyfriend/girlfriend game.

Her gaze was wary, but she didn't slip away. She stayed right with him, moving step for step. Her eyes glittered, not just with anger, but with a curiosity she couldn't quite hide.

Finn flashed a wicked grin and didn't stop until her back connected with the wall. Bending to her, Finn's mouth settled over hers, a warm demand. He didn't touch her anywhere else. Left her plenty of room to push him away if she wanted.

Her lips were tight and stiff for several seconds, but like magic, within moments she was melting against him. She went up on tiptoe, trying to get closer. And her hands gripped his biceps hard, dragging him in. Her mouth opened, the tip of her tongue sweeping across the seam of his lips.

Finn let out a groan of his own, opening and sinking into what she'd offered.

His palm settled against the curve of her cheek, his thumb slipping across the line of her jaw and angling her chin higher.

Her skin was damn soft, her mouth warm, reminding him of somewhere else he'd like to sink deep. God, the taste of her was the best aphrodisiac he'd ever had. Instead of quenching the thirst he'd been fighting, that one taste only made him crave more. Damn, this wasn't smart.

Finding a flash of willpower somewhere buried deep, Finn uncovered the strength to pull back. He dropped his forehead against hers, feeling the soft flutter of her breath brush across his throat. He fought for…something. Sanity. Integrity. Something other than the demand beating a rhythm through his body, urging him to take more.

Pulling back, he stared into her dazed eyes, unable to fight the curl of satisfaction that rolled through his belly. He'd done that to her. With one mind-blowing kiss.

"Damn, woman. If the men in this place knew how amazing that mouth was, there's no way in hell they'd ever leave you alone."

TUCKER YANKED OUT of Finn's arms. Her heart thumped erratically. Her belly writhed with nerves and an energy she hadn't felt in a very long time.

In fact, she'd grown accustomed to not letting herself feel.

Something else rolled through her, too. A bolt of anger that had her hand flashing out and her palm connecting with Finn's cheek. The smack of skin on skin echoed through the empty bar, the shock of contact reverberating up her arm, zinging straight through the top of her skull.

"Shit." Why had she done that? "I'm so sorry, Finn."

If guilt wasn't spreading through her like a bad case of chicken pox, she might have thought the shock that left his jaw slack was funny. It really wasn't.

He stepped away from her, a deliberate movement that took him out of range for round two. Not that there'd be one.

He rubbed his cheek, the gentle *scritch, scritch, scritch* of his stubble sending a tingle down her spine.

"Let me get you some ice." It was the least she could do.

He stared at her for several seconds before his entire body started shaking with laughter. The sound of it rolled out of him, a little rusty and rough. She liked the timbre of it. Like he didn't use it often and it was a privilege that he was sharing the sound with her.

No, she wouldn't let it get to her.

"It isn't funny," she said, barely controlling the urge to stamp her foot. She'd slapped the shit out of him and he was laughing?

"I beg to differ. Can you imagine telling this story to our grandchildren? About swapping ice for our injuries the first time we met?"

What? Tucker blinked, panic and confusion tumbling

around inside her. "Whoa there. No one said anything about grandchildren. This is a pretend relationship."

"So you *are* going to do it?"

Tucker sighed. How the hell had they gotten to this point? Not five minutes ago this man had had her backed against the wall with his tongue down her throat and her mind blank with wanting him.

Beneath her breath, Tucker swore. Finn heard it anyway. She could tell by the tiny quirk to his lips. Damn, she wanted to feel them again. To really savor the moment this time, instead of being blindsided.

Nope, she needed that like she needed a hole in the head.

"I don't have much choice, do I? But I do have one demand. You can't bring Duchess into the bar."

His eyebrows creased together, wiping away his jovial expression.

"She's the reason I was asked to do this, Tucker. Without her there's no point in me being here. I need her to scent your customers for traces of drugs."

"No." She wasn't budging on this. "I can't have your dog running around my bar, freaking out the patrons."

"She didn't bother anyone last night."

"She bothered me. And having her here after throwing y'all out last night would only raise everyone's suspicions."

Finn threw his hands in the air. Beside them, Duchess stirred and Tucker couldn't stop herself from skittering in the opposite direction. Yes, she hated to admit that the dog scared her. But that was the reality.

"Then I might as well not even be here."

Tucker shrugged. "Okay. Sorry I couldn't help more."

She could practically hear Finn's molars grinding

together with frustration. The muscle in his jaw ticked and the vein in his neck throbbed.

"Tonight. I'll agree to leave Duchess home tonight, but we're going to revisit this issue."

"You can revisit it all you want, but I'm not changing my mind. She isn't a service dog, Finn, and doesn't belong in my bar."

She could tell he wanted to argue more, but was smart enough to realize it wasn't going to get him anywhere. "We need to talk about the rest of it, then. Your staff needs to believe that we're a couple."

"Good luck with that. They were all here last night and saw the sparks flying between us."

"So we use that to our advantage. Some of the fieriest relationships stem from passionate hate."

Yeah, not in her experience. As far as she was concerned, any relationship that started out rocky was most likely doomed to failure. Actually, most relationships were doomed to failure, period.

"My team know me a little too well to believe we'd suddenly be together after only one night."

"So we play things a little slow for the next couple days. I hang around, which is really the point of me being here in the first place. You gradually spend more and more time with me."

She really didn't want that, either, but there wasn't much she could do to prevent it. Unless she wanted to refuse to cooperate and have her security team toss him whenever he showed up—and they'd want to know why. Much simpler just to let him spend a few days at her bar, realize he was mistaken about what was happening here and finally leave her alone.

"Fine. But no more kissing," she said, pointing an

accusing finger in his direction. Better to set the ground rules right up front.

"There's one thing you need to know about me, Tucker," he said in a silky voice that sent electricity shooting down her spine. "I never lie. So I can't promise that. Not only do we need to make this look good, but I *want* to kiss you again."

Tucker's body reacted with conflicting responses. Her lips parted and tingled, as if he'd already made good on the promise. Anxiety, desire and wariness tangled in her belly.

She didn't know how to manage Finn McAllister, and that realization floored her. She'd grown up the only daughter of a disciplined military man, with the expectation that she could—and should—take care of herself. She was strong and independent. She'd never met a problem or person she couldn't handle.

But Finn set her outside her comfort zone. Given any other set of circumstances, she would've simply walked away.

He took a step closer and it took everything Tucker had not to retreat. She refused to give him that satisfaction.

Wrapping his hands around her biceps, he bent so he could meet her gaze straight on. "Someone is using your bar to sell drugs, Tucker. This isn't a game."

Her entire body went tight. "I'm well aware of that, Finn."

"The cover is for your benefit. To keep you out of danger. And hopefully prevent any backlash once we zero in on our prey."

Beautiful. Because there hadn't been enough issues to worry about with him lurking around her bar. Now, she was genuinely worried about pissing off some dangerous people, something that hadn't occurred to her until just now.

The back door to the bar opened, the heavy wood panel slamming against the wall, making her jump.

"Tucker?" Wyatt's voice rang out a split second before he appeared in the doorway.

"Too late to change your mind now," Finn whispered, low enough that only she could hear.

"I was hoping…" Wyatt's steps faltered as his gaze landed on Finn. "What's he doing here?"

Tucker shrugged. "His wallet fell out of his pocket last night when he was scooping me up off the floor." She refused to say he rescued her. She'd been perfectly capable of getting herself out of the middle of that mess…once her head stopped ringing. "He stopped by to see if someone had turned it in."

Wyatt's gaze narrowed. "Did they?"

"Lucky for me, someone was a good Samaritan," he picked up her lie a little too smoothly, holding up a slim leather trifold he pulled from his back pocket.

"Yeah, lucky," Wyatt said, drawing out his words. "No one mentioned a lost wallet to me."

"Oh, yeah, well, I found it beneath one of the tables last night when I was closing up. Was going to have you call him when you got in today, but he showed up, instead."

Wyatt's gaze swung between them. It was obvious he didn't necessarily buy the story. But he wasn't suspicious enough to actually call her on it.

Finally, his gaze settled on her. "He try something?"

"No." How the hell did he know that? "Why do you ask?"

"Because he has half a handprint across his left cheek. You might be small, but you pack a hell of a wallop."

Finn's lips twisted into a half grimace, half grin. His fingers rubbed against his cheek again. "You've got that right."

Tucker's face flamed hot. She couldn't remember the last time she'd blushed. Growing up, her dad had always been rather blunt with her about life. Few things embarrassed her. Even fewer once she started tending bar.

Wyatt stared at her like she'd just grown a second head.

Finn let out a soft chuckle. "She and I have been sparking off each other since the moment we met. Let's just say I wanted to know if those sparks might be more than irritation."

Wyatt eyed Finn for several seconds. "And are they?"

Finn shrugged, an impish expression crossing his face. "The mark on my face came about a minute after the kiss ended. What do you think?"

Tucker watched Wyatt's gaze travel slowly up and down Finn's body. Her head of security catalogued every inch, all his strengths and flaws, and finally said, "Interesting."

"Isn't it?" Finn said.

"Okay, boys. You can both stop talking like I'm not here. You," she pointed to Wyatt, "can get to work."

"Yes, ma'am," he said, a smirk curling his lips as he gave her a mock salute.

"Don't make me tell Michelle what a prick you were being."

"Won't be news to her."

"I'm sure."

"You." She pointed to Finn.

"I'll just run Duchess home and get her settled. But I'll be back in a bit."

"Goodie," she mumbled under her breath. Maybe while he was gone she'd manage to get her wayward libido locked down and her brain back in control.

5

THE BAR WAS even busier than it had been the previous night. In addition to the mechanical bull and the armadillo, on Saturdays the Kentucky Rose boasted a local country band. They showed up a little after nine, setting up their equipment on the small stage next to the dance floor. Around ten their guitars started wailing and the low, smooth voice of their lead singer—a female who held the crowd in the palm of her hand—immediately had everyone's attention.

The place filled up fast; it was standing room only within no time at all.

Finn simply kept his spot at the far end of the bar, the seat he'd purposely chosen because of its perfect view—not only of the customers filling the place, but Tucker's staff as they moved through the bar.

He had to give it to them, they were all efficient at their jobs. The girls knew exactly how to play to the crowd—both men and women. They effortlessly served drinks, handled rowdy customers, slapped wandering hands and still managed to make every patron smile.

As much as it bothered him, he'd given in to Tucker's

demand—for now—and taken Duchess home before the Rose opened. He understood her argument that keeping Duchess with him would only raise her staff's suspicions.

She wasn't wrong, but eventually everyone would have to get used to Duchess being there because she couldn't do her job from home.

"You're back."

The redhead from last night wandered up to him, brushing against his arm as she bent over the bar to grab something on the other side.

He wasn't stupid. She'd done it on purpose, the tiny shorts covering her rear riding up and flashing the lower curve of her ass. It would have been easy for her to walk to the other side of the bar to get whatever she'd wanted, but she hadn't.

"Yep. Tucker's a hard woman to ignore." Might as well lay the groundwork for their cover story…not that his words weren't one hundred percent true.

She laughed, a low, throaty sound rolling through her chest. Pressing her back against the dark mahogany, she maneuvered herself right up against his thigh. "I'm Nicole, by the way."

"Nicole, I'm going to save us both some time and say I'm not interested."

He wasn't in the habit of hunting in bars, but he wasn't usually immune to beautiful women tossing themselves at him, either. Tonight, though, it was easy to turn her down.

And not just because he was pretending to be involved with her boss.

"Don't you have customers, Nicole?" Tucker asked, walking up behind the other woman.

Her whipcord voice rocked through Finn and he

didn't bother fighting the smirk that twitched across his lips. Damn, what was it about that smooth, authoritative tone that drove him crazy?

He was used to being the one in charge in every relationship he'd ever had—as short and sweet as most of them had been. He was the alpha in every aspect of his life, not just his job.

Tucker wasn't the kind of woman who would come to heel because he issued an order.

And that made his blood sing.

His gaze found hers over Nicole's shoulder. Her deep blue eyes burned with irritation. That only made his grin widen.

"Yes, ma'am," Nicole said, scooting back into the crowd. He didn't even watch her leave.

Leaning across the bar, Tucker hissed at him. "If you're going to hit on my girls all night you might as well walk out the door right now."

Taking advantage of the opportunity she was unwittingly giving him, Finn shot up, his bar stool scraping across the wooden floor. At the last second she realized what he intended and started to pull away, but not fast enough.

Finn wrapped his hands around her arms and held her in place. Pressing up and over the bar, he bridged the gap between them.

"Kitten, the only woman I'm interested in tonight is you," he said, loud enough for several people around them to hear.

Her lips, bright and glossy again, parted. Her pupils dilated and her skin took on the faintest rosy hue.

God, he wanted to sweep every glass off the bar, spread her out across the smooth surface and uncover every inch of her delectable body. Nope, it wasn't going to be difficult to pretend he was interested. And then some.

Although the display he was about to give was mostly for the staff watching, there was no part of him that regretted what he was about to do.

Cupping the back of her head, Finn brought their mouths together. It was a quick kiss. A promise. A display. Unfortunately—or maybe fortunately—nothing about the kiss felt fake.

Before she could form a protest—or take back the ground he'd just gained by slapping him again—Finn let her go. The heels of her boots clicked back onto the floor. Reaching up, he swiped his thumb across her bottom lip, cleaning the smear he'd caused.

"Now, get back to work," he murmured. "The sooner you're done here, the sooner I can take you out for something to eat."

Tucker blinked at him, her gaze still a little unfocused. "You know we don't close until two a.m., right?"

"So our choices will be limited. I'm sure we can find some greasy spoon that's serving eggs, bacon and pancakes."

Her eyes flashed and a smile tugged at the corner of her lips. He saw it, even if she tried desperately to suppress it.

"Eggs, bacon and pancakes, huh?"

He shrugged. "That's what you do when the girl you're attracted to owns a bar and works strange hours. You make time whenever she's available."

"Jesus, you're a menace," she grumbled, turning away.

"Maybe, but you like me anyway," he hollered as she disappeared into the back hallway behind the bar.

She didn't bother turning, just stuck her hand above her head and flipped him off.

God, she was entertaining.

But there was that voice in the back of his head whispering caution. He didn't really know her...and couldn't discount the possibility that she was involved in this mess.

Snagging his stool, Finn pulled it back up to the bar.

"Well, that was interesting."

He hadn't noticed the woman propped up against the wall a few feet away until she spoke.

She was wearing the trademark Kentucky Rose T-shirt tied in a knot above her belly button, showing off dark mocha skin, toned abs and a glittering ring. Her tight, ripped jean shorts hugged her curves and bright red boots topped off the outfit.

He hadn't noticed this girl last night.

Grabbing the beer he'd been neglecting for the past twenty minutes, Finn took a huge sip before setting the glass down and asking, "What was interesting?"

"All of that," she said, waving her hand between him and the other side of the bar. "You either move fast enough to be classified a superhero, or there's something else going on here."

Well, hell. This woman, whoever she was, was too smart for her own good. Finn knew there'd be people he and Tucker had to work to convince. Apparently she was going to be the first.

"I hear she threw your ass out last night. Twice."

Finn couldn't quite stop the grin that tugged at his lips whenever he thought of the expression on Tucker's face when she'd told him to get out. "Yeah. Yeah, she did."

Dark brown eyes stared at him for several seconds,

studying. Drilling. "So, what are your intentions with my girl?"

"Oh, this is that kind of conversation. Well, I'll be honest and say I don't really know."

Her wide mouth turned down.

"Yet," he qualified. "I mean, we just met." But the best lies were grounded in truth so he found himself adding, "I know I can't stop thinking about her. She irritates and intrigues me at the same time."

The woman chuckled, the sound deep and rich, as she pushed off of the wall. "Yep, that's our Tucker. She's sharp as a tack and won't hesitate to prick you."

Boy, wasn't that the truth. "God, she's brilliant."

Tucker reappeared behind the bar, hauling a rack full of clean glasses. His instinct was to jump up and offer to help her, which he started to do. But he was smart enough to stop himself before the words left his mouth.

Leaning into the bar beside him, the woman drawled, "You're pretty smart yourself."

Rubbing over the spot where Tucker had slapped him, he said, "What can I say? I learn fast."

Staring at him for several seconds, she finally held out her hand and introduced herself. "Monique."

Taking it, he said, "Finn."

"Nice to meet you, Finn. Her daddy might be in Florida, but Tucker has plenty of family here. I've got my eye on you."

His lips quirked up. "Do whatever you feel you need to. But I've got my eye on her, so…"

"Mmm," she murmured, right before Tucker popped back over to his end of the bar.

"Don't tell me this one's bothering you, too." She smacked a towel down onto the bar with a huff. "Do

I need to make a damn announcement that you're off limits?" Tucker's eyes narrowed, crinkling at the corner. "Monique, do I need to remind *you* that you have a husband and baby son at home?"

"Not on your life. Just looking out for you, Tucker."

Tucker growled and flung a wet bar towel at Monique.

Monique grabbed it and tossed it back down onto the bar.

"Watch this one. He's slick," she said, hooking her thumb in Finn's direction. "But yummy and probably worth the hell he's liable to put you through. Something tells me he'll be a good time in bed."

"Monique," Tucker groaned, but the other woman had already turned on her heel and was sauntering away.

Tucker's annoyed gaze found his. He shrugged. "I am damn good in bed."

GOD, HER ANKLE hated her. Tucker groaned as she eased the boot off her foot. An unbidden sigh of relief rushed past her lips as she rested against the dark wood at the end of the bar, letting all her weight settle on the other leg.

Strong hands grabbed her around the waist from behind. Her first instinct was to fight, but that only lasted for the split second it took her to realize Finn was the one holding her.

When had she become so in tune with him that she recognized the feel of his hands on her?

She half expected him to pull her into his arms and kiss her again.

She wanted it.

She didn't. Or, at least, she didn't want to want it.

That stunt he'd pulled at the end of the bar had left her brain feeling like mush for at least an hour.

That recovery time was too damn long for her productivity. Not to mention her sanity.

Then he picked her up like she weighed next to nothing and plopped her down onto one of the bar stools.

And then dropped to his knees.

"What are you...?"

She didn't even get the entire question out before his fingers were probing her ankle, rubbing gently and easing the ache.

And another groan broke through.

His fingers dug into the arch of her foot, releasing the pressure that had built up there. God, it felt good. Tucker dropped her head back, not even caring that her back was pressed into the hard edge of the bar. Whatever Finn was doing felt too amazing.

And he didn't stop at her foot. Slipping the other boot off, he dug into the muscles of her calves, turning them to jelly. The liquid burn was amazing.

"You're good with those fingers."

Tucker didn't even realize what she'd said until Finn looked up at her from his position at her feet. His green eyes blazed. She felt the hit of them straight to her belly and below.

Her legs weren't the only thing going liquid and warm.

He didn't even have to voice the words for her to know exactly what he was thinking. Because she was thinking the same thing. Her sex throbbed and she wanted the relief of his fingers there, as well.

Finding strength from somewhere, Tucker pulled

her good foot out of his hold, placed it on his shoulder and shoved.

He barely budged, but it was enough to get her point across. For a second, she thought he was going to ignore her, leaning in instead of pulling back.

But slowly, reluctantly, he gave in, putting space between them. Not that it helped much. Her entire body was already buzzing with energy that she had no outlet for.

Scooting off the stool, she dropped her feet to the floor and nearly crumpled when her bad ankle couldn't hold her up. She would have hit the ground if Finn hadn't caught her.

"Easy there, kitten."

She needed to shake him off before she did something stupid. Shrugging his hands away, Tucker grasped at anything to distract herself and put some space between them.

"Do not call me that."

Finn just crossed his arms over his chest, pressing close and looming over her. Which only irritated her more. God, she missed her heels. Being short was such a disadvantage. Especially when staring down a big, bad military man with a penchant for ignoring anything she said.

"I'm serious."

"Oh, I know you are," he said, humor tingeing his words and ramping up her frustration.

"I'm not your kitten, your sweetheart, your darlin' or anything else. I'm nothing to you, Finn McAllister."

"Whatever you say." He shot her a look that was clearly meant to placate her. She wasn't buying it. The man was entirely too irritating—and enticing.

"I don't suppose you'd let me carry you out to my Jeep?"

"Not on your life."

"Thought you'd say that. Well, put your boots back on, then, and let's get this show on the road. Don't know about you, but I'm starving."

Tucker pulled in a deep, calming breath when he moved away. Rounding the bar, he stopped long enough to scoop up the glass he'd been using and pop it into the built-in industrial dishwasher before disappearing down the back hallway.

Sinking onto the stool behind her, she leaned forward to pull the boots onto her feet, but ended up pressing her palms to her flushed face, instead.

Get a hold of yourself.

It's the advice she would have given anyone in her position. Finn McAllister flustered her, and not in a good way. After a childhood of being jerked around like a kite, Tucker went out of her way to be the only one in control of her life…and her body.

At the moment, those same sensations of being tossed and untethered were welling up and she didn't like it.

Okay, that wasn't entirely true. Her body enjoyed the buzz of energy Finn drummed up with a single charged look. But that was just physical attraction. She watched it every single night, with a front row seat to the mating dance of the human species.

And she experienced the flip side of it, as well, when she had to mop up tears along with the condensation off the bar whenever a customer came in to drown their relationship sorrows in alcohol.

Nope, none of that was for her. She didn't want the high, because she didn't want the low. Wasn't worth it.

Her resolve back in place, Tucker pulled the second boot on and eased herself to her feet. She felt more solid, in control.

At least, until she crossed the bar to find Finn checking all the doors and locks. Safeguarding her bar.

Dammit. She really didn't want to like this man. On top of wanting him, that would make keeping him at arm's length so much more difficult.

6

FINN HELD THE door open. Tucker scooted under his arm, trailing that tempting scent that was uniquely her—a combination of woman, whiskey and rose—right beneath his nose.

The tendrils of her blond hair brushed across his arm, so soft. He wanted to bury his hand in it again.

But this wasn't the time or place. Tucker had her armor firmly back in place, something he'd recognized the minute she straightened from putting her boots back on.

Maybe it was better that way.

But he wanted to rip that veneer away again. The need burned through him, hot and heavy.

"Finn!" His name rang out above the din in the all-night diner, the scent of grease overpowering everything else when he stepped inside.

Tucker stood in front of him, shifting on her feet. Gorgeous, completely put together, even at 3 a.m., and a little out of place.

From behind the long counter, Patty waved at him, her salt-and-pepper hair pulled up into a ponytail high on her head. "Sit anywhere, sugar. I haven't seen you in ages. Where's that dog of yours? I've got a treat for her."

Finn cut a pointed gaze at Tucker. "*Someone* made me leave her at home."

Patty gasped and harrumphed.

Tucker threw up her arms. "Why does everyone act like *I'm* the crazy one for thinking a dog doesn't belong in a bar and a restaurant? I'm sure she's perfectly happy chewing on your slipper or something."

"Duchess does not chew on anything."

"Except bacon. I'll wrap her up some. You take it home," Patty said. "Y'all sit wherever."

Settling a hand on Tucker's hip, Finn ignored the way she jumped as he steered her toward a booth at the back.

Normally, he preferred the counter so he could chat with Patty, but tonight that wasn't his goal.

The place was busy, even at this hour. Or maybe it was the hour that made it busy. Everything else in the area was closed.

He waited for Tucker to take the other side before sliding onto the red vinyl that afforded him a view of the door.

Patty appeared at the end of their table a moment later.

"Well, who is this, Finn? She's pretty, although she doesn't seem to like our girl, much. I'm reserving judgment for the moment. What can I get you two?"

Finn was used to the no-nonsense and one-sided way Patty carried on a conversation. She finally took a breath and let him answer.

"Tucker Blackburn, I'd like you to meet Patty Warren. Tucker owns a bar on the outskirts of town, the Kentucky Rose. Duchess and I are working on her. I'd love to hear your opinion, but with this one I'm not sure it'll make a difference."

Patty squinted at him for several seconds. "Like that, is it?"

He shrugged. He'd known Patty for years. His dad used to bring him to this diner when he was a kid, father/son bonding time. Patty had been behind the counter, even then.

Stepping back, she let her gaze travel slowly over Tucker, taking in everything about her. Patty was almost as unforgiving as his camera lens could be.

After several seconds, she said, "The Kentucky Rose, huh? Never been, but I've heard good things."

"Thank you," Tucker said, smiling up at Patty. The smile was genuine, which only made him like her that much more. Some people might've dismissed Patty, assuming she was nothing more than a short-order cook. But what the woman could do with eggs and a bowl of buttermilk batter was nothing short of miraculous.

"We met at Tucker's bar. There was a scuffle."

Patty smacked him across the shoulder. "Now what have I told you about getting into trouble, Finn McAllister?"

Tucker laughed, the sound deep and throaty. "He wasn't the problem. Well, he was. And then he wasn't. Actually, he came to my rescue when I got knocked on my ass. Just waded into the middle of a fight, picked me up off the floor and made sure I was okay."

Considering he'd had to pull a thank-you out of her at the time, hearing the humor and gratitude in her voice made something deep inside him hum.

"Yep, that's my boy. He's got a heart of gold." Patty snapped the order pad she'd been holding against the edge of the table. "Maybe I can forgive you for sending Duchess home, after all."

"Gee, thanks," Tucker said, cutting him a wry grimace.

With a single nod, Patty dismissed the entire conversation. "What'll you have?"

Finn didn't hesitate. "Two loaded omelets, two big stacks, home fries for two, coffee—and you wouldn't happen to have some ibuprofen handy, would you?"

Tucker's mouth flattened into an unhappy line. Her eyes flashed that brilliant blue fire that made him want to push her just so he could see them glitter.

"Water. No coffee," she corrected. "And could you bring me some peanut butter?"

Patty grinned, wrote on her pad and spun on her heel.

Crossing her arms in front of her, Tucker leaned into the table. "Maybe that's not what I wanted to order."

"Maybe it wasn't. But it's what you should have wanted. And since you've never been here, I wanted to give you a taste of the best. If you don't like it you can order something else."

"That would be rude."

Finn laughed. "Since when does being rude bother you? You haven't hesitated to put me in my place any chance you get."

"That's different."

"How?"

"You deserved it. Patty's done nothing but be an unwitting accomplice to your highhanded tactics."

What was it about this woman that stirred his blood? She was intelligent and confident. She didn't hesitate to give him a piece of her mind—or anyone else who deserved a dressing-down, for that matter. She intrigued him and challenged him.

Which only made it damn hard to remember that he shouldn't be letting her in. He was supposed to be playing a part, not actually falling for her. Not to mention there was a very real possibility she was up to her pretty little neck in this mess. God, he needed to remember that.

Patty plopped a glass of water, two mugs with coffee and a couple of little brown pills onto the table. "If anyone asks, you didn't get those from me," she said, before disappearing again.

Tucker stared at the steam rolling off the surface of her mug. She glared at him for several seconds, groaned and then snatched up three packets of sugar. Whacking them against her palm, she dumped them, along with a couple of creamers, into the cup before stirring. "If I can't fall asleep tonight I'm gonna call you repeatedly and hang up whenever you answer. Fair warning."

Finn hid his grin behind the rim of his own cup. "With all the shit you just dumped in there, does that even qualify as coffee anymore?"

Her eyebrow quirked up. "Ask me if I care."

Finn settled back against the plush cushions, stretched his arm out over the top of the booth and watched her as he sipped.

He needed more information about her. Something that would help him determine which side of the line she fell on—good or bad, involved or innocent.

Tucker stared back, meeting him beat for beat. She didn't flinch or hide. She simply stayed steady and waited. Patient.

Lowering his coffee back to the table, Finn said, "So, I understand you have an MBA."

Now her body flinched. If he hadn't been watching he might have missed her reaction. What he didn't understand was what had prompted it. Most people would be happy to discuss earning their master's degree.

"Yeah. How'd you learn that?"

"All part of the job, kitten. You don't think we ran a background check on you?"

Tucker shot him a look. "Do I want to know what else you know about me?"

Probably not. "I know enough."

"What the heck is that supposed to mean? I don't like the idea of you having details about my life, Finn. Details I haven't shared with you."

"Give me your ankle."

"What?"

Waving his fingers at her, he said, "Give me your ankle. And tell me something I couldn't learn in any report."

Reluctantly, Tucker slipped her foot up onto the seat of the booth beside him. Shaking his head and subverting a grin attempting to spread across his lips, Finn grasped the heel of her boot and eased it off. Wrapping his fingers around her ankle, he gingerly lifted it until her foot rested on his thigh—as elevated as he could get it at the moment.

Scooping the medicine up off the table, he handed it to her along with the glass of water. "It's been long enough that you can take more."

Tucker stared at him for several seconds, but finally reached out and took the pills. "Thanks."

More often than not, she seemed to be the one taking care of everyone and everything—her staff, customers, and every last detail at the bar. Finn got the impression she wasn't used to anyone taking care of her.

Which only made him want to do it all the more—not because she needed it, but because she deserved the same care and attention.

"Are you going to answer me?"

Tucker turned away, glancing out over the diner like the people around them were suddenly fascinating. "Not much to tell."

It was obvious he'd made her uncomfortable.

"That's a lie. You're one of the most complicated and interesting women I've ever met. But even if that was true, I need to know the little details. The things you'd share with a new boyfriend. Your family. Your childhood. Your hopes and dreams."

She didn't want to answer his questions. Finn wondered if that was just the way she was—overprotective and closed off—or if her reluctance was exclusive to him.

Either way, he could understand and identify. He'd never been an open book, but his time overseas had made him even more reluctant to let people in.

His experience with Bethany had left him floundering. He'd been wrapped up in his own life, blind to what she was dealing with, and he'd missed the signs she was in trouble. He'd never forgive himself for that. But then he'd been assigned to the K9 team and received his orders to specialize in uncovering drugs. Most soldiers he served with were unaware of Duchess's special training, and keeping them in the dark made his job both more and less difficult. But he'd felt he had a purpose. An opportunity to atone for his mistake and save someone else.

He'd been vigilant, trained hard and put everything he could into the job. But that still didn't prevent him from being blindsided one evening in the barracks when Duchess alerted him to drugs hidden in the belongings of one of his best friends.

That story had a happy ending because the man had gotten the help he'd needed. But Finn had lost a friend.

He'd begged Finn not to turn him in. He'd promised that it was just recreational, to take the edge off when things got to be too much. He hadn't had a choice.

He could still clearly remember the rage and betrayal on his friend's face. He'd been forced into a treatment program, though, and was now clean as far as Finn had been told.

Patty plopped their plates down in front of them, pulling him out of the unpleasant memory. "Enjoy."

Tucker spun her plate around, as if she was trying to decide which angle to attack the omelet from. She did the same with her stack of pancakes, moving the butter to the side of her plate and spreading peanut butter between the layers before dousing the entire thing with a river of syrup from the warm carafe. The sweet scent of maple filled the space between them.

"Don't think this gets you out of answering my questions."

She glanced at him from beneath her lashes, a wide grin spreading across her luscious mouth. "Oh, I wouldn't dream of it."

Finn just shook his head. "Peanut butter?"

"Ever tried it? No? Don't judge until you have."

Finn hadn't even bothered to glance at his food. Watching Tucker was too entertaining. She attacked her plate with the same energy she did everything else, cutting off a large bite and shoveling it into her mouth.

Her eyes closed and a loud moan rolled up from her chest. His body responded as if he'd caused the sound instead of the food.

She chewed, swallowed and then looked him square in the eyes. "Okay, you were right. These pancakes are amazing. I didn't realize how hungry I was until just now."

Without waiting for his response, she went back to annihilating her breakfast. Finn ate his own, a little more slowly because he kept getting distracted by the sight of her.

In the middle of it, she held out a bite of peanut-butter-covered pancake for him to take. There was something intimate and comfortable about the way she did it, grabbing more food for herself from the fork they'd just shared without batting an eye.

The way she relished each bite was...arousing. He wondered if she'd savor every moment with him the same way.

No, scratch that. He knew she would, because he wouldn't accept anything less. He wanted to carry her off to the nearest bedroom and indulge every whim for the next handful of hours.

Instead, he finally said, "It's sharing time, kitten."

"What?"

"Reprieve's over. Tell me everything I need to know about you."

SHE HAD BEEN STALLING, hoping Finn would get sidetracked and they'd end the night without her having to give him anything further.

He'd already stolen two kisses, making her bones melt in the process. He was at a distinct advantage because apparently he had a nice little report on her entire life. She couldn't imagine what else he wanted to know about her.

But just the fact that he was asking left her uncomfortable.

The problem was, she wasn't entirely certain if that reaction stemmed from being forced to share pieces of herself when she wasn't ready—or the fact that it was *him* asking the questions.

She'd had relationships over the years, but none of them had truly mattered. She'd purposely picked guys who weren't really looking for anything more than what was on the surface.

When she did get involved with someone, it was on her terms. She decided when she wanted to begin something, and then when she wanted to end it. She picked guys who were easy and wouldn't ask too much of her, men who would satisfy her physical itch, but not require anything else.

Finn definitely did not fit into that category.

He was demanding. Arrogant. Opinionated. Gorgeous and powerful. Honorable. Sweet, although he tried very hard not to let anyone see that.

She didn't want to answer his questions because doing it felt like opening a door she'd never be able to close again.

It felt like a risk.

And while she had no problems taking risks with her business and her livelihood, she didn't take risks with her heart. She'd learned a long time ago to be satisfied with being alone. It was easier. Safer.

She had no desire to let anyone into the details of her life. But Finn wasn't content with that. She could ignore him now, but he'd either dig up the answers on his own or keep pestering until she got so irritated the answers exploded out of her.

Maybe he'd leave her alone if she gave him a little something.

"Fine. I'm a military brat. Raised by my dad. He was Air Force. My mom left when I was little. Don't really remember her. And I don't really care to since she decided her needs were more important than our family.

"When my dad was deployed I'd stay with an aunt in California. We didn't exactly get along. She never wanted kids and resented being stuck with me, even if she always told my dad she was happy to have me.

"I've lived all over the country, but no place was really home. Until San Antonio. I was old enough and decided to stay when my dad moved on from here. Went to college. Tended bar. Created a business plan, inherited some money, opened the Rose. The rest is history." Tucker leveled her gaze at him. "Satisfied?"

"Hardly." He grinned at her. "But it's a start."

It was more than a start. It was all she intended to give him. Her entire life story condensed down to a few sentences, a handful of words. There was a part of her that thought it pathetic she was able to do that. But the rest was a little proud.

She refused to make her life into some sob story. Everyone had hardships. She was hardly the first girl to have a parent walk out. Or the first military kid left a little scarred by the constant moves and fear that she'd be left an orphan, depending on someone who didn't really want her. She'd overcome those things and refused to let the past define who she was now.

"Why Kentucky Rose?"

"It's my full name. My dad was from Kentucky and my mom's name was Rose."

There were days it bothered her she carried even that small piece of her mother. And she'd hesitated to use it for the bar. But then she'd realized using it made that piece of her into something good instead of a reminder of someone selfish and destructive.

Before Finn could pepper her with more questions, she decided it was time to turn the tables. "How'd you get involved with the K9 unit?"

If she hadn't been watching him, she might have missed the way his mouth tightened for the briefest moment. Or the flash of pain that shot through his eyes.

"I joined the Air Force straight out of high school. My parents couldn't afford college and I goofed around too much in school—didn't qualify for scholarships. So, the military offered me the best options. My plan was always to put in my time, get out and go to college. Be an engineer or accountant or something."

"Sure, because you're a nine-to-five, suit-and-tie kinda guy." No way did that fit. "So what changed?"

Finn's arm shifted against the back of the booth. To anyone else watching, he probably looked comfortable and relaxed. But even after only a couple of days, Tucker recognized the evidence of tension drawing his body tight.

His gaze traveled around the restaurant. She was used to him cataloguing their surroundings, but this was different. Almost like he was searching for an escape instead of a threat.

"My sister died of an OD. Meth."

Tucker sucked in a harsh breath. That was not what she'd expected. The pain the memory caused him was clearly etched into every line of his face.

Reaching across the table, she grasped his hand and squeezed. "I'm so sorry, Finn."

Here she'd been lamenting her own sob story when he had one much, much worse. Yes, they'd both lost someone, but she hadn't known her mother, not really. Only missed the idea of her instead of the reality.

Finn had lost someone he'd loved very much. Far too tragically and far too young.

"Thanks." He flipped his hand over, snagged hers and wove their fingers together. Man, he wasn't one to overlook an opportunity.

Tucker felt a zing of energy travel up her arm and down her spine. But that was soon overcome by a spreading warmth when his thumb began to gently brush across the top of her hand. Over and over, in a mindless rhythm.

"Why are you so afraid of my dog, Tucker?" His voice was smooth and hypnotic. She'd bet it was the same tone he used to calm Duchess down when she was wound up.

She really didn't want to answer his question, because doing it would give him more insight into her psyche than she wanted to give him. Finn McAllister was already too keen for his own good.

But she also couldn't very well ignore the question. He deserved to know why she didn't want Duchess at the Rose.

Taking a deep breath, Tucker tuggd her hand away from his. "When I was young, maybe six, seven? We lived right outside the base in a small house in North Carolina. You know, the kind crammed right on top of each other. Our backyard wasn't big, but my dad tried to make the best of it. One of the reasons he picked the house was because of the amazing swing set in the backyard." Just the memory of it had a smile flitting across her face. She remembered being so excited about that house. Thinking that maybe it would finally feel like home. "It had a twisty slide, a built-in sandbox and a turret just like a castle."

"A little girl's dream castle."

Picking up her napkin, Tucker began to pull it into tiny strips. "Yeah. But there was this huge dog in the yard next door. He had this deep, growling bark. And every time I came outside he'd spend the entire time just snarling at me through the fence. He'd claw and dig. Jump so that his beady black eyes could see me.

"My dad promised he couldn't get to me, but I wasn't so sure. It got so bad that I started refusing to go outside, which only made my dad angry. Not that he yelled or anything, but I knew he was disappointed."

The worst feeling in the world had been disappointing her father. He was all she had.

"One afternoon, it was late spring so the weather was perfect, Dad forced me to go out there. I didn't want to, but I didn't want to see him upset so I went. And, as usual, the dog growled and barked. Jumped. And then everything went quiet. I thought maybe the neighbors had let him into the house or something. I was so happy. Until I went down the slide and saw him waiting at the bottom."

Tucker glanced up at Finn, taking in the stark line

of his beautiful mouth. It was obvious he found the story unsettling.

"I ran. He chased. Knocked me down, ripped a hole in my jacket. Luckily my dad came running out before he could do more damage."

"He did enough."

Her lips quirked up at the corner in a half smile that held little humor. "True. Little dogs I can deal with. But big dogs…"

"Like Duchess."

She nodded. "Like Duchess. I don't like them. Logically, I realize they aren't all like the one that attacked me, but…."

Reaching across the table, Finn placed his hand over hers, stopping the motion of her fingers that she hadn't even been aware of. Somewhere in the middle of her story she'd started shredding the strips of napkin into little pieces until there was a small pile of white fluff on the table in front of her.

A blush flamed up her skin, the heat of it scorching through her.

Finn didn't seem to notice or care. He simply twined their fingers together. "Thank you for sharing that with me, Tucker. I promise Duchess is the most well-behaved dog you've ever met, highly trained and obedient. I won't lie and tell you she's harmless because she isn't. But I swear she would never take anyone down without the proper command."

Tucker shrugged. What was she supposed to say to that? "Okay." It didn't really matter. Duchess was only on the periphery of her life because Finn was currently occupying it. But in a few days, or weeks, that would end and his dog wouldn't be an issue anymore.

Releasing her hand, he nodded at her plate. "Finish your breakfast and I'll take you home. You must be exhausted."

She could argue with his order, but she really was tired and the idea of going home and falling into her bed held merit.

So what if the brief thought of Finn joining her flashed through her mind? She squashed it immediately—well, almost immediately.

Cleaning her plate only made the need for sleep worse. Now that she was full and sated, other needs were pushing to the forefront.

Finn didn't even bother to argue about who was going to pay the bill. He snatched up the ticket as soon as Patty set it down and walked over to the counter to pay. Tucker opened her mouth to protest, but decided the least he owed her was food.

He'd pretty much turned her life and livelihood upside down today.

Climbing into his Jeep, she said, "Drop me back at the bar so I can pick up my car."

"Nope. Not happening. It's late. You're tired. You shouldn't be driving with that ankle. I'll take you home."

Irritation spiked through her. "Your heavy-handed tactics are really annoying. How the hell am I supposed to get to work tomorrow without my car?"

Finn didn't bother answering her. He just slammed her door shut and strolled around to the driver's side like they weren't in the middle of a debate. He took his sweet time settling into the seat and cranking the engine before turning to her. "I'll come pick you up. What time do you need to be in?"

"That's silly. I'm perfectly capable of driving myself to work. I've been doing it for years now."

"Never said you weren't. But we're supposed to be a couple and there's no way I'd let any woman I was dating drive home when she's this tired."

Tucker growled, the sound matching something she would have expected from Duchess.

Assuming the conversation was over, Finn put his Jeep into reverse and pulled out of the lot. Tucker crossed her arms over her chest and turned her body toward the window.

"You don't know where you're going and I have no intention of telling you."

This time his laughter scraped down her spine, and not in a good way. "Kitten, I know about your MBA. You don't think I know your address?"

She wanted to scream. The sound rumbled up through her chest and threatened to erupt from her throat. Somehow, she managed to push it back down. Gritting through her teeth, she said, "If you call me that one more time you're going to get a matching handprint on the other cheek."

He flashed her a little-boy grin that had the flustering effect of making her insides turn to mush, ratcheting up the urge to knock some sense into him at the same time.

"I get it. You're into kink. Not a problem for me, kitten."

This time, she didn't stop the shout of frustration. His ensuing chuckle only made her want to yell louder.

7

HE WAS AN IDIOT. Not because he'd made her angry, but because he found her anger arousing as hell. He liked it when her eyes sparked and her skin flushed.

He liked her spunk and fire. It lit him up.

But it probably wasn't smart. So Finn let her stew all the way to her home.

He was surprised to find she owned a small brick raised rancher on the back side of a quiet neighborhood. He had no idea why, but for some reason he'd pictured her living in the middle of some trendy downtown square filled with twenty-somethings who liked to party.

This place reminded him more of PTA meetings and soccer club than whiskey and rockin' country music.

He pulled into her driveway and killed the engine. "What time do I need to pick you up tomorrow?"

"I'll find my own way."

"Nope." That wasn't going to happen. "It's better if we arrive together, anyway."

"So everyone thinks we slept together just days after meeting?"

"Well…yeah. That's kinda the idea, Tucker. We need people to believe the story we're telling and part of that charade is that our relationship is moving fast."

"Too fast," she muttered under her breath.

Finn's lips twitched, but he managed to keep the grin tucked away.

"So, what time should I stop by?"

"Ugh!" She dropped her head back against the seat. Her eyes closed and her shoulders rose and fell on a deep breath.

What he wanted to do was take her inside and tuck her into bed. What he did instead was sit patiently and wait for her to realize what he was suggesting was the smartest move.

"I don't usually wake up until one or two. I try to get to the bar between two and three."

"Okay, I'll be here at two. Give me your phone."

She rolled her head without lifting it from the headrest and tried to glare at him, but her expression had little impact. Her entire body was weighted down and dragging.

Surprisingly enough, she didn't argue with him, simply unlocked the phone and flipped it into his lap. Finn snatched it and entered his information. "Text me if you're ready earlier. Chances are Duchess and I will be up and out already."

"Not much for sleep?"

"No." That was a bit of an understatement. He'd never needed much, but since his time in Afghanistan, he'd found it hard to sleep through the night.

Tucker opened her mouth, no doubt to press the issue, but snapped it closed again instead. Just as well. He would have answered her questions—he had no intention of keeping anything from her that she wanted to know—but neither of them were in the right frame of mind for that conversation tonight.

Gathering her purse, Tucker pushed open the door and dropped her feet to the ground. Finn waited for her at the edge of her walk as she fished out her keys.

"Jeez, you don't know when to quit, do you?" she grumbled. Moonlight splashed across her face, illuminating her in a way that made her features soften.

He stuffed his hands into the pockets of his jeans. It was either that or kiss the hell out of her. "Nope," he said, rocking back on his heels.

Following her up the walk to the front door, he watched her hand extend and push the key into the lock. But the door opened before she'd even turned it, the hinges creaking ominously.

Shit. A sick sensation rolled through the pit of his stomach.

"There any chance you left your door open before going to work tonight?" he asked, his words even and deliberate.

"No."

Snatching her by the shoulders, Finn spun Tucker behind him, instinct taking over.

"Go back to the Jeep." He really wished Duchess were here. Her search skills would have been useful right about now to ensure the intruder wasn't hiding somewhere inside Tucker's home. "Call 911 and tell them you need to report a break-in. Then call Dade and Simmons and tell them to get their butts over here."

Her palms flattened against his shoulder blades. He could hear the sound of her harsh breathing. Felt the way her fingernails dug into his skin. All he could think about was the story she'd shared with him earlier, the echo of the fear she'd felt as a little girl still so clear and strong.

He needed to reassure her. "You're fine, Tucker. I promise I won't let anything happen to you."

"Yeah?" she ground out behind him. "Who's going to protect the bastard who broke into my place? If they've taken anything or destroyed my home you better hope they're not still inside. If I find them I'm ripping someone a new asshole."

Laughter wheezed out of his constricted chest, easing some of the tension that had been building there, unchecked. Tossing a glance at her over his shoulder, he took in her pinched expression and the rage glittering through her gorgeous eyes.

Okay, so she wasn't upset or frightened. Upon reflection, Finn had no idea why he'd expected her to react that way. Maybe because many women who weren't military or police would have.

But he knew Tucker wasn't afraid to take on a fight. Last night and the bruise on her cheek were proof of that.

"Pull back those claws, kitten, and do what I've asked, please. I don't think anyone's still inside, but I'm not taking that chance. I'm going to investigate."

"Please tell me you have a gun in the truck. I'll get it for you."

He did, actually, although he had no intention of using it. But he'd grab it anyway, just in case.

"Yep, under the driver's seat."

Tucker's warmth disappeared from his back. He could hear the gentle click of her boots against the pavement as she hustled to the Jeep.

A few minutes later Tucker said, "Here," holding out his pistol. "I'll make the calls. Just…" her gaze flitted down his body and back up again "…just don't get yourself hurt, all right?"

His mouth twitched. "I'll be fine, kitten." Then Finn pushed open the door and disappeared into the dark house.

HELL, SHE DIDN'T like watching him leave. Tucker's heart was frantically trying to beat its way out of her chest. Anxiety and anger coasted along every nerve, making her irritated and jumpy.

She called 911 and reported the incident. They were dispatching someone right away. Declining the operator's offer to stay on the line until an officer arrived, she hung up and dialed Dade from Finn's contact list.

"This had better be damn important, McAllister." His voice was groggy and unhappy.

"Well, I suppose that depends on whether or not you deem my house being broken into important. I know I certainly do."

"Ms. Blackburn?" The half-asleep quality to his voice disappeared. Tucker had this mental image of him bolting straight up in bed. She hoped he was single, otherwise his wife had just gotten a rude awakening. "Where's Finn?"

Tucker crossed her arms and stared at her open front door. It was dark. Pitch black. She normally left a lamp burning because she came home in the middle of the night and it was always nicer to return to a welcoming glow.

Until that moment she hadn't registered that the light was even out. Hell.

"He's currently scoping out my house to make sure no murderers or rapists are lurking in the closets. When we got home my front door was unlocked and left open."

"And you're certain you didn't forget to lock the place before leaving?"

"Yes, I'm religious about locking my doors at night, Officer Dade."

"Okay." The sound was muffled, as if he was running a hand over his face while he talked. "I'll be there in ten. Fifteen at the most."

"Great. You can join the officers 911 is sending out."

A stifled groan echoed down the line right before it went dead. Tucker stared at the open door for several seconds, debating before deciding she'd had enough. She wasn't the kind of woman who sat around waiting.

Walking up to the door, she pushed it wide open and yelled into the darkness. "Finn, I'm coming in. Don't shoot me."

From the back of the house she heard a single curse word. A few seconds later Finn appeared on the other side of her living room.

"I called Dade. He's on his way along with whoever 911 is dispatching."

"Great. It looks like whoever was here is gone."

"Beautiful."

"Take a quick look and let me know if anything is missing."

Tucker let her gaze travel around her living room. The high-end TV she'd bought less than two years ago was still hanging on her wall. Maybe it was too heavy? Knickknacks, throw pillows and every DVD she owned littered the floor, but nothing appeared to be missing.

Walking through the kitchen, down the hall, she entered her office. Papers were scattered all over the place, a real mess she didn't even want to think about cleaning up. But the laptop she used as her home computer still rested in the docking station and the dual monitors set up on the desk were right where she'd left them.

Every room she checked was much the same. Stuff was everywhere, a few things here and there broken. But nothing was missing. She should have been relieved. She wasn't.

Especially when she ended in her own bedroom, staring at her precious collection of couture shoes thrown haphazardly around the room. "Bastard," she growled beneath her breath.

"Excuse me?"

Turning, she wasn't surprised to find Finn leaning against the frame of the door leading to her bedroom.

"You heard me. Whoever did this—" she swept her hand around the mess "—is nothing but a bastard. And if he so much as left one scratch in the fine Italian leather I'm going to be out for blood."

"I'll warn Dade," he drawled. "You know you have a problem, right?"

Tucker's eyebrows creased. "What are you talking about?"

He nodded his head towards the mountain of shoes spread out at her feet. "I'm no expert, but doing the math, you could wear a different pair of shoes every day of the year and still not duplicate any. I'm pretty sure that means you have a problem. I'd be happy to help you find a support group."

Tucker glanced around, taking in the beautiful vision of all those shoes. And felt her lips twitch. He wasn't wrong. She had a bit of an addiction, but she could afford it and it wasn't hurting anyone.

Turning back to him, she shrugged. "I already belong to one. We meet at least once a month. To buy new ones."

Finn just shook his head, pushed away from the door and strolled straight into her domain. He didn't stop until he was standing right in front of her.

She could feel the delicious heat of him. She had to crane her neck backward to look up at him, something she didn't particularly enjoy, normally. But with him, it didn't bother her.

Especially when his hand cupped the back of her head and his thumb brushed across the curve of her jaw.

He stared at her for several seconds, to the point that her body began to burn and she had to fight the urge to squirm beneath his scrutiny. He made her feel uncomfortable and alive all at the same time. How was that even possible?

"You okay?"

"Yeah." The answer was automatic. Tucker didn't even bother to stop and think about it. She was always okay.

But Finn didn't let her get away with that. "No. Are you okay?" he asked again, drawing each word out.

This time, she took several seconds before answering. Was she? Really?

"Yes. I'm irritated. I mean, there's a part of me that feels violated. I've worked hard for this place. It's the first house that's really felt like mine. That someone just thought it was okay to break in and ransack it for their own purposes really pisses me off." Wow, she hadn't realized how much those words were true until they tumbled from her mouth. "And the fact that they didn't take anything makes it worse, doesn't it?"

The hand Finn had been resting gently on her waist tightened for the briefest second. It was answer enough, but his words confirmed what her brain already knew. "Yeah. If the place had been stripped clean we could at least hope the break-in was coincidental. But considering nothing of value appears to have been taken, it's a good bet that whoever it was came looking for something specific."

The drugs they'd found the other night? "This seems pretty extreme for a bag of meth."

"Maybe."

It was obvious Finn didn't really agree, but didn't want to argue with her considering the mess they were standing in.

"Searching the bar would make more sense than tearing apart my house."

"Who says they didn't search the bar?"

Tucker's back slumped against the wall. Until that moment she'd been living on the hope that whatever was going on, none of her staff were involved. The people she employed had become her surrogate family and it hurt to think that any of them could be using her place for nefarious purposes.

"Dammit," she breathed out.

"It's all right." Finn pressed his forehead to hers. "We'll figure this out. You're not alone."

The simple words, brushed across her mouth from the warm heat of his breath, ricocheted through her. They offered comfort, but also ripped and hurt, somehow opening old wounds that had never quite healed.

She didn't want to feel anything for this man, but couldn't seem to stop it from happening.

It felt like she'd been alone for a very long time. Forever, really. Sure, she'd had her father growing up, but she couldn't really count on him considering he wasn't around for large chunks of time.

Without thinking, Tucker pushed up onto her toes, sealing her mouth to his. She needed that physical connection to another human being—to *him*—more than anything else in that moment.

The kiss was unexpectedly soothing, draining away the tension that had infiltrated her body. It was easy and sweet. *Real*. Just for the two of them and not part of some show for an audience.

Oh, there was an underlying heat, but they purposely kept it banked. Now wasn't the time. The flash of red and blue lights splashing across the wall of her bedroom was proof of that.

Pulling back, Finn brushed his thumb over her still tingling lips. "Time to face reality."

THE BRIGHT PINK and orange of dawn were just starting to paint the sky when the officers finally left. While Dade and Simmons spoke to Tucker and directed the forensics team they'd called in, Finn slipped away to pick up Duchess. He'd wanted her there, offering any little bit of protection she could.

The team dusted for prints, but found none. Whoever had done the B and E had been smart enough to wear gloves, at least. He and Tucker had done the best they could to triage the mess after being given the all clear. What was left could wait until later.

In the morning—or later that morning—Finn had

every intention of speaking to Tucker about installing a security system, including cameras to record all entrances. Even if she didn't want to keep those measures in place after this was all over, until then, it would make him feel better.

Maybe he should have the system installed first and ask for forgiveness later.

"So, chances of me being up early today are nil. We better make it three. I won't have the brain power to tackle paperwork this afternoon, anyway."

"Not a problem. We can head in whenever we're both up and ready. Just point me in the direction of your spare sheets so I can lay them out before crashing. I'm dead on my feet."

Tucker stared at him for several seconds, blinking slowly like he'd just grown a second head and it might disappear if she waited long enough. She was adorable when she was speechless.

"Uh, you are not staying the night."

"Uh, yes I am. There's no way I'm leaving you here alone." At least not until he got that security system installed. "I'm not suggesting we sleep together, Tucker. I'm too damn tired. The first time we have sex I want to be one hundred percent so we both enjoy the hell out of it."

He certainly enjoyed the way she pulled in a harsh gasp, her pupils dilating. Behind the unforgiving constriction of his jeans, his dick stirred. *Nope, down boy.*

"I barely know you and you want to sleep in my spare bedroom?"

She was searching for any excuse. God, for a woman so strong and uncompromising she could certainly be skittish.

"Tucker, you know me better than you apparently realize. There are men I've worked with for years who don't know about what happened to my sister. Women that were in my life for months didn't get that part of me, either. So, stop stalling, get the sheets and let me get some sleep. Please."

Tucker blew out a breath, her bangs fluttering with the motion.

"Unless you really would prefer we sleep together. Fair warning, I sleep in the nude."

Turning on her heel, she shot out of the kitchen and up the stairs. Finn followed, a little slower, his feet dragging against the pale wooden floor. Pausing at a closet, she yanked it open, grabbed a set of sheets and shoved them into his stomach.

Finn doubled over, grasping them. He snaked an arm around her waist, pulling her tight against him, too. "You know where to find me if you change your mind," he whispered into her ear.

Tucker pushed against him so he let her go. Her palms smacked into his chest. "God, you're a pain in the ass, you know that?"

"So I've been told."

Finn watched her try to stomp down the hallway while favoring her bad ankle. The slam of her door echoed through the house. And he couldn't hide the smile curving his lips anymore. It was so easy to push her buttons. He should probably stop it. Especially considering that the more time he spent with her the deeper she dragged him into wanting her.

And not just for one night.

Looking down to where Duchess sat at the bottom of the stairs, Finn simply shrugged. He dropped the sheets on the floor and went back down, making a circuit of the house to double check that all the doors and windows were secured. He'd done that with the officers once already, but he wouldn't be able to sleep if he didn't do it again.

Confident that everything was as tight as could be, he told Duchess to curl up on the sofa in the living room. He'd set out bowls of water and food for her earlier. Normally, she slept in the same room with him, but he wanted her downstairs, their first line of defense should whoever broke in show up again.

It took him about five minutes to put the sheets on the bed, dump the pile of decorative pillows and smothering comforter into a corner and strip. Finn let out a sigh of relief when he finally crashed onto the soft mattress.

He was out within minutes.

8

SHE COULDN'T SLEEP. It was so stupid. She was exhausted, her body so tired that she physically ached with it. But her mind just wouldn't stop spinning.

Crystal meth. In her bar.

The role she'd agreed to play and the way it made walking away from Finn impossible. He made her nervous. Uncomfortable. Hell, he stirred all of her senses and made her want.

Which only made the lie she'd told him when he first found the drugs worse.

Then there was the break-in.

She wasn't naive enough to think drugs had never found their way into the Rose before. Her team had caught kids popping ecstasy in the bathrooms once or twice. Another time, they'd even found some asshole trying to slip GHB into a woman's drink. And she had no doubt some patrons walked in the door high.

But she'd been secure in the idea that her team was at least keeping dealers from using her place as their turf.

And the break-in only made her realize the problem was bigger than she'd first thought.

It was probably too much to hope that the incidents were coincidental. The timing was too perfect. She really wished Finn had been wrong when he hypothesized someone had come looking for their stash. But she really didn't think he was.

Not that it mattered. The result was still the same—Finn was right now down the hallway, sleeping in her guest bedroom.

Finn. God, he was so irritating and amazing. Protective and infuriating. Sexy as hell with that dangerous edge that she always seemed to find attractive.

The story he'd told her about his sister...it had broken her heart. And explained so much about the man who had steamrolled his way into her life.

She was honestly impressed by the way he seemed to have handled the tragedy. He'd taken the worst moment of his life and turned it into a driving force. A purpose.

But he was so dictatorial and commanding. Like she needed that in her life. She was too strong and independent to deal with that kind of bullshit. Like him demanding to stay at her place.

Okay, so there was a part of her that appreciated the reassurance of knowing he was down the hall. And, as much as Duchess made her skittish, she had to admit that knowing she was downstairs—she'd heard Finn tell her to stay—helped settle her nerves.

Maybe she should give in to whatever this was between them, let the pent-up energy find an outlet. And hope that it burned hot and bright and then disappeared.

And, God, the longer she lay there, staring at her ceiling in the dark, the more her body buzzed with the need to do just that. She wasn't normally the kind of woman to be ruled by her libido. But right now, she couldn't seem to get a grip.

She was restless and edgy, her mind spinning uncontrollably.

Damn him for kissing the hell out of her. For waking her up and making her want. For sending that flare of need shooting through her body.

All she could think about was what would've happened if they hadn't been interrupted. She had no doubt that Finn McAllister knew his way around a woman's body. He'd proven that with just his mouth. Tucker couldn't imagine what he could accomplish with his hands and that long, thick ridge of an erection in the mix.

No, that wasn't true. Her imagination was pretty damn good—capable of sinking any good intentions she might have.

She wanted him. It was that simple. Finn had made it clear he desired her. Who knew how long they'd have to play this little charade?

The reality was she'd barely survived one day without caving. Eventually, her body would overrule her head. Better to be in control of the capitulation than to explode into a messy situation that might feel damn good, but would end hella complicated.

Besides, tonight, after everything, she didn't want to be alone.

Before she could change her mind, Tucker bounded out of bed. Her feet smacked the floor, ankle twinging a reminder that she was still injured, and she padded down the hall.

She didn't bother knocking on the closed door. It was

her damn house. And if she found him already naked that would just make things that much easier.

Pushing the door open, Tucker's gaze shot around the dark room.

"Tucker?" His voice came at her, a low, deep pulse running through the single word.

Closing the door behind her, Tucker let her body sag against the hard panel. Her hand was still a fist around the knob...just in case something changed her mind.

"Hey. What's wrong?" She heard the shift of the blanket and sheets. Saw the shadow of him as he rose from the bed. "I promise you're safe. Duchess is downstairs guarding the place. If anyone comes back they'll have to get through both of us before they get to you."

Out of the darkness, his hands clasped her shoulders.

And that was all she needed.

Grabbing for him, Tucker went up onto her toes and somehow managed to find his mouth in the dark. His muffled sound of shock ricocheted through her, but wasn't nearly as devastating as the groan that followed. She wasn't even sure if the sound was his or hers.

Heat suffused her, flashing up from the bottoms of her feet to consume her in a flame that was so strong. She hadn't felt this way in a very long time. Maybe ever.

Tucker's hands raced across his chest, over his shoulders, across his ribs. She encountered the waistband of his boxer-briefs and realized he'd been lying when he said he slept naked. Wasn't that a shame.

Curling her fingers into the band, Tucker went to yank them down, but before she could, Finn's hips shot back. His mouth disengaged and his hands tightened around her shoulders, holding her at arm's length.

"Whoa, kitten. Take a breath."

"I don't need to breathe," she panted, each word a gasp that echoed in the throb between her thighs.

"Maybe not, but I do. This is one hell of a one-eighty. Yesterday you slapped me, tonight you're ripping my clothes off. What's changed?"

"Nothing. No, everything. I don't know."

Tucker squeezed her eyes shut and begged her brain to clear so she could make sense. Dropping her head back, she let it bang against the door.

"You've been trying to get in my panties since we first met, Finn. Are you telling me now that I'm offering you're turning me down?"

"Hell, no. Right now I'd give anything to have you flat on your back in that bed, coming apart beneath me while I thrust deep."

"Yes." That's what she wanted.

"But, despite what you apparently think of me, I'm not the kind of man who takes advantage of a woman who's just been thrown for an emotional loop." Reaching up, his fingertips slipped across her cheek, tangling in a piece of hair that had fallen over her shoulder. He tucked it behind her ear, his movements soft and gentle.

No. That wasn't what she needed. Not right now. She needed wild passion. She needed exhaustion so her brain could shut off. She needed for her body to feel something—everything—so the rest of her could just…be.

"You're not taking advantage. I'm a big girl and I know what I'm doing. Tonight, that's all that's on the table. I don't want more. Not with a man who demands more than he asks. Not with someone who has no problem forcing his way into my life."

His lips ticked up in the smallest of smiles. "Kitten,

the only man you'd let into your life is one that blasted his way through those walls you've built sky high. And, trust me, I'm more than happy to give you a physical outlet whenever you need one, but not tonight. And not like this."

Tucker growled in the back of her throat. Embarrassment at his rejection rolled up through her chest. Her skin flushed warm. Thank heaven for the darkness hiding her humiliation.

Tucker tried to move out of his grasp. Her hand, still tucked against the small of her back, tried to turn the knob. But Finn wasn't letting her go and the knob wouldn't cooperate.

"Oh, no, you don't."

Without asking permission, Finn bent and scooped her up into his arms. It was only a few steps from the door to the bed. He set her down, but almost before her back hit the mattress she was scrambling up again.

"What do you think you're doing?"

"Giving you what you really need." Finn landed on the bed beside her, wrapped an arm around her waist and used the weight of his own body to pull her back down onto the bed.

Stretched out behind her, he tucked her small body into the shelter of his big one. His legs tangled with hers, holding her hostage.

Tucker struggled. This was not what she'd had in mind when she'd decided to go to him. How had this gone so terribly wrong?

Sure, she didn't have a lot of experience seducing men, but she had a front row seat to the best training ground there was. She thought for sure she'd learned enough to get the job done.

Apparently not.

His fingers swept her hair out of the way, exposing her neck. She could feel the warmth of each breath
across her skin. The solid weight of him at her back.
He surrounded her. His heat. His scent.

His strength.

"It's okay, Tucker. I've got you."

His words, whispered into her ear, broke something
inside her she hadn't realized was dammed.

A shudder rolled through her, shaking her entire
body from toes to crown. And then she relaxed, every
muscle just…letting go.

"That's it. You're strong for everyone else. For yourself. There's no weakness in leaning on someone every
once and a while."

"Says the big, bad military man." She attempted a
chuckle, but the sound came out broken.

"Have you seen my dog downstairs? She's an extension of me. I depend on her. She depends on me. It's a
two-way street."

"She's an animal, Finn."

"Don't tell her that. Sometimes I'm convinced she
thinks she's human. Who do you let in, Kentucky
Rose?" he asked, brushing his fingers down her arm,
to tangle with her fingers.

No one. She let no one in. And that was the way
it was going to stay. Because people left. Moved on.
Change was the only constant in life and she knew
herself well enough to realize she didn't handle it well.

"Go to sleep. If you still want sex in the morning,
we can talk. Or not talk…"

Inexplicably, a grin curled across her lips. "Bastard."

She felt his shrug, but he said nothing more.

And, to her utter surprise, this time, when she closed her eyes, her brain didn't spin. Instead, exhaustion pulled at her and she was asleep in seconds.

FINN WOKE UP to an inferno. It rolled through his gut and throbbed at the center of his soul.

No, wait, that was his dick.

There was a warm body draped across him. Silky hair tickled his chin and chest. The soft, subtle smell of a woman filled his lungs. And his hand was currently curved around a naked hip.

Tucker. She was curled against him, taking up all the space and making him burn.

Cracking his eyes open, Finn surveyed the situation.

Somehow, his hand had worked its way beneath the waistband of Tucker's shorts, hence the handful of her naked skin. God, it was so smooth and warm.

He should probably do the right thing and pull back. But he wasn't going to. She'd come to him last night. Yes, she'd been begging for one thing while really searching for another. But...

Tucker's eyelids fluttered. Her body shifted, making him groan when her hip grazed against the stiff erection currently begging him to take what he so desperately wanted.

The dark pink tip of her tongue flicked out over her lips right before her incredible blue eyes popped open.

The sleepy, dreamy expression on her face nearly killed him. Paired with the slow, sexy smile that curled her lips... He was only human.

"Morning, kitten."

The space right between her eyes puckered adorably. "Don't call me that," she murmured, her voice rough with sleep.

Unable to resist, Finn dipped his head and claimed her mouth. The kiss was easy, lingering. Just the brush of his lips against hers over and over again until he felt the rush of her sigh caress his open mouth.

Finn pulled back, searching for some semblance of honor, but she pursued, taking and deepening their connection.

"Nope," she said against his mouth. "More."

"Are you awake, Tucker?"

"Yes." The single word pressed into him, making his skin buzz.

"Are you sure?"

"Mmm," she hummed, stretching her body. Sharp hips and soft breasts rubbed against him in all the right places. "I don't think I've ever been this awake in my life. Touch me, Finn. Now."

Filling his hands with her blond curls, Finn cupped the back of her head and held her still while he stared into those brilliant blue eyes for several seconds. He searched her gaze, for any sign of the uncertainty, fear and confusion she'd possessed last night. The reason he'd said no when his entire body was begging him to say yes.

Last night, she'd wanted something quick to take the sting out of everything that had happened. And any other time he might have been willing to give her what she needed.

But he'd known after ten minutes with her that he wanted more from Tucker Blackburn than a quick tussle between the sheets. She was the kind of woman who made life interesting and entertaining.

Instinctively, Finn knew she'd be like a Roman candle, all spark, sizzle and beautiful flash of burning light. He wanted it. All of her. And once would not be enough.

This first time wasn't going to be quick. He needed to savor every second and sensation. Every inch she agreed to share with him.

Tucker stared back at him, certainty, understanding and a twinge of disquiet filling her clear gaze. He would have been more concerned if that twinge wasn't there. It told him she realized that this was more than the verbal parry and thrust they'd been exchanging.

That disquiet told him she got it and felt the same kernel of apprehension that he did. Because he wasn't sure he could handle this any more than she could.

But he sure as hell was willing to see what happened. He'd be a damn fool to let her go before they knew.

Trying to alleviate some of the tension curling beneath the surface, Finn let a knowing smirk tug at the edges of his lips.

"God, sometimes I want to smack you," she murmured.

He had no doubt. "I'm sure. But most of the time you want to back me up against a wall and have your wicked way with me."

Tucker choked, "I'm pretty sure you're the one who's got a thing for walls, soldier."

He shrugged. She wasn't wrong. Whenever she was close the only thing he could think was how to get closer.

"Maybe, but this morning I'll settle for tasting every inch of you."

Reaching between them, Finn grasped the lacy edge

of the tank that matched her tiny sleep shorts and tugged until she leaned up so he could pull it over her head.

God, her skin was a dusky rose, warm from sleep. Her breasts were amazing, the dark pink tips of them pearled up and begging for him to taste.

Rolling them both, Finn tucked her beneath him. He found the pulse thudding at the side of her neck and sucked. She tasted like heaven, all heady and sweet.

He trailed kisses down her throat, across her collarbone, sucking, tasting, leaving little nips along her skin.

But Tucker wasn't the kind of woman to just sit and take. She wanted something and had no problems showing him. Twisting her fingers into his hair, she applied gentle pressure, urging him lower.

Finn breathed a laugh against her, trailing the edge of his tongue along the curve of her breast. He circled her puckered nipple, never quite touching where she wanted. Her fingers tightened, skating the edge of pain as she tried to force him to suck her deep inside his mouth.

He wasn't an easy one to bend.

"Finn," she said, the single word a warning he had no problem ignoring.

"Tucker," he countered, switching to the other breast to deliver the same sweet torture.

"Touch me."

"I am." He had a damn hard time fighting the smile she would have felt from blooming across his face.

"Not where I want."

"Mmmm," he rumbled, the nonresponse no doubt as infuriating as his lack of compliance with her demands.

In the end they'd both appreciate that he hadn't listened.

Touching her, tasting her was a treat he intended to fully indulge. Her body was a marvel, all compact muscle and lithe lines. The way she moved intrigued him and had from the first moment he'd laid eyes on her.

He wanted to discover every secret she held...and protect them for her.

Eventually, she realized she wasn't getting anywhere with her demands and changed tactics. God help him.

Releasing her death grip on his hair, her fingers slowly dragged down the back of his neck making a shiver rock through his body. She made a triumphant sound deep in her throat.

Oh, it was on.

And he was looking forward to enjoying every minute of what was coming next.

Her hands trailed along his shoulders, back and ribs. Teasing caresses that barely skimmed over his skin. Strong fingers digging into tight muscles, releasing knots he didn't even realize he had.

And through it all, the more she explored the more his cock throbbed, begging for the relief of being buried deep inside her.

Not yet.

He wasn't done with her yet.

Tangling their legs together, Tucker bucked her hips up, pulled down and somehow had him flipped onto his back before he could pull his next breath.

He hadn't expected that.

But he should have.

She stared at him, triumph laughing down at him from her deep blue eyes.

"Whatcha think about that?"

"Kitten, you can put me on my back anytime you

want if you promise to look at me just like that every time you're above me."

Her hips ground against him, dragging a deep groan from his parted lips.

"How am I looking at you?"

"Satisfied."

"Not yet."

Minx. "Satisfied with yourself. And ready to lick me from head to toe like your favorite Popsicle."

Finn's hands settled on either side of her hips and urged her to keep sliding against him. The friction of their shorts was torture. He wanted her naked. He wanted to push deep inside her. Needed it. More than his next breath.

Any notion of taking his time evaporated.

Urging her onto her knees, Finn helped her pull the shorts down and off. He pushed his own hips up from the bed and enjoyed the slight tremble in her hands as she helped him do the same.

Stretching over him, she fumbled in the bedside table. He hoped to God she was getting a condom, but he really didn't care. Not when the pert little knot of her nipple was dangling in front of his face. Torturing her had tortured him just as much.

Leaning forward, he pulled her deep into his mouth and sucked. Hard.

She gasped and her thighs clamped around his hips. The taste of her exploded across his tongue. Sweet, with a hint of spice running beneath the flavor. Just like Tucker.

On the outside she looked like the adorable girl next door, but on the inside she was one of the toughest women he'd ever met.

Her brain fascinated him just as much as her unbelievable body. More, actually.

And right now he wanted all of her.

Grasping her hips, Finn picked her up and settled her back to the mattress. Her golden curls spilled across the bed. Somehow he managed to rip open the condom and roll it into place.

His fingers found her sex, delving deep to find her slick and hot. She bucked beneath him, whimpering. "Not enough."

"No. Not nearly enough."

A driving need pounded through his brain, deep inside his chest, out to every extremity on his body. The need to be connected to her. With her.

Hooking his arms beneath her knees, Finn pushed her legs up and out, leaving her wide open to him.

Another time he wanted to feast on her, just like this. Spread out beneath him and helpless to do anything but take what he wanted to give her.

But for now...his vision was already graying at the edges, becoming hazy with the single-minded obsession over her.

Tucker watched as he lined their bodies up together. Her hungry, glazed expression was one of the most erotic things he'd ever seen. Or it was until her eyes closed in utter bliss when he thrust forward to fill her.

Blazing heat shot up his spine. "So damn good," he murmured, finding any little section of her skin to kiss and suck.

Her fingers clamped tight onto his shoulder. His hip. His ass. It was like she couldn't get enough of him either, even like this, buried so deep.

After several seconds Finn began to move, pulling

out and thrusting back for more. Over and over again. The drag and plunge of skin. Her little whimpers. The way her body undulated beneath him, chasing after every last drop of pleasure.

She quivered, her entire body racked with tension and bliss. He could feel her winding tighter and tighter, so ready to explode. And he wanted that. Wanted to feel her clamp hard around him, shuddering with the release he gave her.

Reaching between them, he found the tiny knot of nerves buried between the soaked folds of her sex. Two, three hard swipes of his thumb and Tucker completely lost it.

Her mouth opened on a silent cry that never actually found voice. Her entire body strained against him, muscles clamping tight around his cock and making him see stars. It was too much.

His own release exploded up from the base of his spine, avalanching out and burying everything except the way being with Tucker made him feel.

Collapsing onto the bed beside her, Finn rolled, grabbing the edge of the comforter and throwing it over both of them.

He'd deal with the aftermath in just a minute.

Whenever his brain came back online.

9

FINN'S ARM AROUND her waist felt…good. The weight of it was grounding, something she'd needed after he'd made her soar into the stars.

Even now, minutes later, she couldn't quite manage to catch her breath. Maybe that was just a sign she needed to spend more time on the treadmill. Yeah, that must be it.

Her brain was urging her to get up, get away. But her body was still reeling, unable to follow the simplest of commands.

Her guest bed was torn to pieces. Her pillows were on the floor. Her head was at the foot of the bed, resting on the hard shoulder of a man who was more often frustrating than endearing. Not that she hadn't seen the softer side Finn McAllister tried to conceal.

Another time, with anyone else, these things would have bugged the hell out of her. But Finn seemed to crash through all her defenses.

He was a whirlwind.

Whatever.

Groaning at the twinges of protest her body eked

out, Tucker made an attempt to roll out of bed. Finn's arm around her waist tightened, holding her in place.

"Where do you think you're going?"

Anywhere he couldn't make her lose her ever-loving mind and give in to his desires…whether it was a smart idea or not.

"The bathroom."

Finn eyed her, his lids narrowing as his gaze dragged over her face.

"Nope."

"What do you mean, nope? You're in *my* house, Finn McAllister. I'll go wherever I want."

"If that's what you were doing, fine. But we both know it isn't. You're going to hide. To slink off and convince yourself this was a monumental mistake that will never happen again."

"Slink off? Not on your life. I don't slink anywhere." Slinking suggested that she'd done something wrong— something to be ashamed of. And she hadn't. "And this was a monumental mistake. I don't need to lock myself into the bathroom to know that."

"The only problem with what just happened, Tucker, is that we both have things we need to do today and can't immediately do it again."

Tucker harrumphed. There was something about Finn's attitude that both rubbed her the wrong way and inexplicably set her at ease.

With him, she knew exactly what he was thinking. Where she stood. He didn't hold anything back—good or bad. There was something comforting about that.

Especially considering most of her life she'd felt like she was standing on quicksand, never knowing when everything was going to collapse and change. Again.

Although, that didn't mean Finn needed to know that. In fact, it would be better for her if he had no idea. Because something told her, the man wasn't above using whatever advantages he could get.

"Do you always get your way?" she huffed.

"Nope."

"Could have fooled me. Do you have any idea how maddening you are?"

A smile tugged at his lips. "I'm pretty sure you've said that before."

"Because it's true!"

Rolling them both, Finn tucked her beneath him, pressing up onto his elbows until he was staring straight into her gaze. Straight into her.

Tucker tried to look away, but his fingers, buried in her hair, held her in place.

"Tucker, I'm not unaware that our current situation is unconventional. But you fascinate me. And it's been a damn long time since anything or anyone has fascinated me.

"Your fire. Intelligence. Stubborn independence. You do realize that you're just as frustrating, right?"

God, what was she supposed to say to that?

Something very close to bliss bubbled through her veins. The sensation was…tempting. She liked it. Wanted more of it.

But that wasn't safe. Or smart.

Wrapping her hands around his wrists, Tucker pulled until he let her go. "Whatever. This was just sex, nothing more."

"Keep telling yourself that, kitten," he whispered, his mouth ghosting along the edge of her jaw. An involuntary shudder rocked her, outing her as a big, fat liar.

He chuckled. Tucker rammed a fist into his shoulder.

Rolling them both, Finn lifted her up off the bed and planted her feet on the floor. Pointing her in the direction of the shower, he swatted her rear. "Go get ready."

A perverse part of her wanted to stomp in the opposite direction just for spite. But that would have been counterproductive since she really did need a shower.

And coffee.

"Make yourself useful." Pointing a finger at the door, she issued an order of her own. "Make me some coffee. And stop calling me kitten!"

The edge of his lips twisted into a grin. "You see, *kitten*, the difference between us is that it bothers you when I tell you to do something—even if you know I'm right. Whereas I would do absolutely anything you asked of me."

Without waiting for a response, Finn slipped through the door and downstairs.

"The difference is you don't ask!" she yelled.

From down the hallway she could swear she heard the low rumble of his chuckle. So frustrating.

"Don't look at me that way," Finn said, glancing over at Duchess. Curled up in the corner of Tucker's kitchen, the dog stared at him with calm, steady eyes.

"Yeah, I know she's going to make this difficult, but maybe that's part of the appeal. She's going to make me earn every piece she shares, which will only make them sweeter to savor."

Pulling open drawers, Finn searched for the spatula he needed to flip the pancakes he was making. In another pan, bacon popped and sizzled.

"Yes, I will give you some bacon. Don't I always?"

"Are you carrying on a one-sided conversation with a dog?" Tucker asked from the doorway.

Giving Duchess a wary stare, she skirted to the far side of the kitchen, walking the long way around the island to avoid the dog.

This was a problem they needed to solve right now.

Not only was Duchess a major part of his life, but he needed her at the bar and after Tucker's home had been broken into...he didn't have the time or space to back down or take this slowly.

Setting the bowl of batter aside, Finn pulled the skillet of bacon off the burner and set it to the back of the stove.

Grasping her hand, he led her into the living room, calling behind him, "Duchess, heel."

"What are you doing?" she asked, tugging her hand.

He could feel the tension in Tucker's body as the dog brushed past her and moved to her place at his side. It bothered him. Maybe because he knew she had nothing to fear from Duchess. But possibly because it was just sad that she didn't understand the companionship that Duchess—and all the dogs he'd handled over the years—had provided for him.

After learning more about Tucker's childhood, he couldn't help but think that if she'd had a dog growing up she might not have felt so lost and alone.

Stopping at the big wingback chair in Tucker's den, he turned her to face him and placed his hands on her shoulders. "I'm going to introduce you and Duchess to each other."

If he hadn't been holding her, she would have bucked backwards and fallen straight into the chair.

"We've already met."

Squeezing, Finn dipped down so he could look straight into Tucker's dark blue eyes. "I promise, Duchess won't hurt you. Trust me?"

Tucker squeezed her eyes shut, but that didn't stop him from seeing the wheels spinning inside her head. Her body practically vibrated with the need to run, which only made Finn more determined to push her.

"I have every faith in you," he whispered.

The shudder that rocked through her body nearly had him changing his mind. Until her eyes popped open again, this time fierce and full of determination.

"Fine. What do you want me to do?"

The enormity of the faith she'd just placed in him was humbling.

Pushing gently, he said, "Sit."

Tucker's body collapsed into the chair. Finn crouched down beside her, calling Duchess over.

Finn began to rub his hands over Duchess's head, scratching right behind her ears just the way she liked. Bliss filled the dog's eyes. Since she valued praise, this was like her dark chocolate and sea salt caramel treat. Leaning close, he rubbed his face along the side of hers and said, "Be careful with her, girl. She's skittish and afraid of you."

Turning his head to take in Tucker, he said, "Call her to you."

"No." Tucker's gaze was wary and her answer immediate. But before he could say anything, she huffed and changed her mind. "Duchess, come here."

The exasperated way she issued the command made him laugh. "Try it again, this time like you're issuing an order to one of your employees."

Pulling her mouth into a straight line, she said, "Duchess, come."

The dog stirred and moved until her face rested on the edge of the chair Tucker sat in.

"Rub her head."

Tucker reached out her hand. It was difficult to miss the slight tremble as she eased forward. Her fingers barely grazed Duchess's head before she snatched her hand back, cradling it against her chest like the dog had snapped.

Duchess didn't even flinch. She sat quietly, her steady gaze trained solely on Tucker.

"Again. Scratch her right behind the ears and she'll be your best friend."

A sound wheezed from Tucker's lungs, a cross between a laugh and a groan. "I don't know that I want her to be my best friend."

"I think maybe you do. Try again."

This time, Tucker's hand was steady when she reached out and lingered a few seconds longer. She did it several more times before she finally felt comfortable enough to leave her hand there without pulling back.

"Her fur is so soft." Tucker glanced in his direction for several seconds, but her gaze went straight back to Duchess. "She's so...still. And steady."

"Yep, that's one of the reasons I love her. Each dog is like a person. They have their own personality. Some of them are more high-strung. They need energy and motion. Duchess has always been calm. She needs to have a purpose."

"I can understand that."

Of course she could. He'd been watching her for days and one thing was glaringly obvious to him. Tucker valued herself by the hard work she'd put into her business. And she had every reason to be proud.

Confident they were moving in the right direction, Finn stood from where he'd been crouched beside her chair and stretched. Looking down at both woman and dog, he said, "Stay."

Tucker stared up at him, her dark blue eyes flashing fire. The fact that her hand still rested on Duchess's head made something warm clench inside his chest.

"That better have been a command for Duchess."

He tossed her an impish grin. "Whatever you need to tell yourself, kitten," he said, before turning to walk away.

"Wait. Where are you going? Don't leave."

The slide of her jeans against the cushion of the chair followed him into the kitchen. He snatched a couple of the cooling pieces of bacon from the pan, paused long enough to pop one into his own mouth then headed back to the den.

He half expected to find Tucker standing across the room with Duchess still waiting patiently beside the chair. And that would've been okay. Baby steps.

But he was astounded to find Tucker sitting on the floor, her back against the side of the chair and Duchess's head cradled in her lap.

Finn paused. The expression on Tucker's face could only be described as part astonishment, part wonder as she looked up at him. "I fell."

He hadn't heard a commotion, but he didn't doubt her since she was sitting on the floor. "Are you okay?"

"Yeah. I tripped trying to bolt after you. Landed inelegantly on my rear. And Duchess seemed to want to make sure I was okay before settling her head in my lap."

Striding across the room, Finn reached down and picked Tucker up. Setting her back on her feet, he tucked her into the shelter of his body. "Sure you're okay?"

She nodded, burying her head against his shoulder. Finn squeezed. Her reaction was endearing and only made him want to protect her even more than he already did. Which he was smart enough to realize she wouldn't appreciate.

So, instead, he put a little space between them and held out the bacon he'd snagged.

"Time to reward her with her favorite. Tell her to sit."

Duchess, already scenting the bacon, popped up onto her haunches before Tucker could even issue the command. "Praise her and give her the treat, but don't jerk your hand away. Doing that could startle her and her natural reaction would be to chase after the treat she already knows she's getting."

"Okay." Tucker said, "Good girl," and she held out the piece of bacon. She gripped it with the edges of her fingertips, wanting to put as much distance between her fingers and the dog's mouth as possible. And, as always, Duchess was perfect.

Instead of snatching it from Tucker's hand—not that she ever did—she daintily reached out for the end of the bacon and tugged until Tucker let go.

Turning Tucker back to him, he held her at arm's length. "You do realize I'm taking Duchess with us to the bar today, right?"

All of the excitement fled, Tucker's expression closing down. "No."

His grip on her arms tightened. She could be so frustrating. "I understand your concerns, Tucker, but I need Duchess there if I'm going to accomplish anything. You did so great with her this morning. You know that she's well behaved and won't cause any problems in the bar. So what other arguments do you have against her coming?"

Her lips compressed into an unhappy line, Tucker glared at him.

"You know I'm right."

With a grumble, she said, "Fine. But she needs to stay in the front, Finn. No going past the bar into the back. She needs to stay far away from the storeroom, office and kitchen."

TUCKER HAD BEEN brooding since they got in Finn's Jeep to head to the Rose. This was becoming a habit he could do without.

It was obvious she wasn't happy with the turn of events, but that wasn't going to change his stance. She could let it bother her all she wanted.

It was possible she simply didn't like to lose an argument. And, really, he couldn't blame her. He didn't, either. But this one, there was no other choice. Duchess needed to be at the Rose.

Right now, since the bar was mostly empty, Duchess had staked out the most comfortable spot in the place— the padded area around the mechanical bull—and was catching a little nap. Considering she'd stood watch all night at Tucker's place, she'd earned the rest.

From his perch on the stool at the end of the bar, Finn watched Tucker talk to Wyatt. And fought the urge to swat the guy's hand away when he casually slung an arm around her shoulders, letting his fingers tangle in her hair.

It was obvious they were close. Finn's male instinct

said *too* close. But watching Tucker, it was apparent she didn't respond to the other man the way she did to him.

Where as she was easy and fluid with Wyatt, every time she got within ten feet of Finn, emotional energy sparked between them. The difference was obvious, although that didn't seem to matter to the predatory male instincts currently pounding through him.

Though he was smart enough to realize the issue was his own to deal with, and clamped down on the urge before doing something stupid.

"Nothing was taken?" Wyatt asked.

Shaking his head, Finn dialed back into their actual conversation.

"No, not that I could find."

"Did you maybe interrupt the burglary? Scare them off?"

Pushing up from the stool, Finn sauntered closer. It helped allay some of his restlessness when Tucker shifted away from Wyatt and toward him. The other man's arm dropped from her shoulder, easing his own tension even more.

"No. There was no one there." Just the thought of what might've happened if he'd let Tucker go home alone like she'd wanted made him shiver. Needing the reassuring feel of her against him, Finn eased her into the shelter of his body, settling his arm across her waist. He was rewarded when she melted against him. Was she even aware she'd done it? Probably not. "Whoever broke in was long gone before we got home." Thank God.

"Home?" Wyatt lifted a single eyebrow. "Making yourself pretty comfortable there, aren't you?"

He shrugged. "I've never seen the value in hesitation. When I see something I want, I take action to get it."

Tucker twisted, frowned up at him. Her irritated expression was rather endearing. "You make me sound like the first place ribbon at the county fair. I am not some trophy to win, Finn McAllister."

Finn brushed his lips across her forehead. "You're absolutely right," he murmured. "You're like a photograph of the most gorgeous landscape. The kind of art that evokes a riot of emotion. Something to be savored and admired."

"Yeah, that's not much better."

He just flashed her a knowing grin.

Wyatt eyed him suspiciously. It was clear the other man didn't quite trust him, which was just as well. It was good to know Tucker had people other than himself watching out for her.

"So, they were looking for something? Any idea what?"

Tucker opened her mouth. He had no doubt she was about to let her head of security in on the story of him finding the drugs and her working with him and the task force.

Which was exactly what Finn wanted to avoid.

While there was a possibility the dealer was a regular, it was more likely the person was an employee. At the very least, there was almost definitely an inside man. Someone feeding information and looking the other way.

It didn't escape his notice that Wyatt was in the perfect position for both things. Even though their informant had told them he'd bought from a woman, that didn't necessarily mean she was working alone. Finn wasn't ready to mark anyone off the list.

Well, except for Tucker. He was trusting his gut on

this one and really didn't think she was involved. Yes, he was ignoring the tiny voice in his head that said he didn't *want* her to be involved, but right now it felt like a safe bet.

Besides, either way, the quickest way to ruin their operation was for the wrong person to learn the real reason he was hanging out at the Rose.

"No ideas," he cut in, gently squeezing Tucker's waist in a silent warning.

She frowned, but didn't contradict him. She did shrug away, though, leaving his palm to tingle where he'd touched her.

"I'm tired of speculating. We'll probably never know who broke into my place."

"Are the cops at least making an attempt?"

Wyatt was awfully interested in not only what had happened last night at Tucker's place, but also the cops' plan to find the culprit. Just understandable curiosity in his capacity as Tucker's head of security, or digging for more information because he was responsible and wanted to know what they knew?

"Yeah, but without any prints to run..." Tucker shrugged.

Monique called to Tucker from the other side of the bar where several other members of the staff were gathered. Apparently they met a couple of times a month before the bar opened just to all touch base and go over anything pertinent.

From where he sat perched across the bar, it looked like Monique was the ringleader. She was clearly close to Tucker and took on the second-in-command roll whenever Tucker was busy with other things.

Tucker threw him a side-long glance and walked

away. Finn didn't even try to hide his interest as she did. Why bother? He blatantly stared at her ass. He loved the way she moved, all fluid energy and grace.

"Stop staring at my butt," she yelled without turning around.

"Not on your life, kitten," he countered with a chuckle. A twitter of responding laughter rose from the group of women.

How long before he could get his hands on her again? He wondered just how much coaxing he'd need to do to get a quickie in the back office. She was wearing a tiny pair of shorts that barely covered the curve of her ass. He was pretty sure she'd worn them just to taunt and tease him.

It was working.

He could imagine sweeping everything off that tiny little desk of hers and bending her over it, the sound of her whimpers, groans and sighs as he made that overactive brain of hers shut down and her body light up.

"God, I can't stand here and watch this," Wyatt's voice growled beside him.

Finn didn't bother to look at the other man. "Watch what?"

"You eye-fuck her from across the room."

Laughter rolled through his chest. "Then you'd best go find something else to occupy yourself with, because I have no intention of stopping. Tucker Blackburn is one amazing woman and I'm going to appreciate her any chance I get."

"The only thing saving you right now from getting a fist to the face is Tucker's reaction to you."

That did get his attention.

"What do you mean?"

Wyatt's gaze narrowed. "I've known her a very long time and I've never seen her let a man touch her, let alone relax into him the way she just did with you. That's earned you some breathing room, but know I'm watching you." Wyatt didn't even wait for his response before walking away.

Finn couldn't help the thrill that Wyatt's words shot through him. He wasn't normally the kind of guy who worried about the men who might have come before him, but with Tucker everything seemed to be different.

And it mattered, knowing she was different with him. Probably more than it should.

From across the space, he watched her interact with her staff. She was intent and animated, although he couldn't quite hear what she was saying. She commanded respect and attention, earned it from the team she managed. It was clear, from the way the women around her responded in kind, that Tucker didn't rule with fear or threats. She did it with competence and understanding. Clear direction and expectations.

Heart.

That's what she had.

Something sharp lanced through his chest. A need to be in that inner circle. A drive to be the recipient of her attention and care. Tucker might have steel walls a foot thick around her heart, but something told him when she finally let someone in…they were there for life.

He wanted that.

A buzz distracted him. Reaching into his back pocket, Finn pulled out his cell and groaned when he saw Simmons's name on the screen.

Glancing around, he disappeared down the back hallway, away from anyone who might hear his side of this conversation.

"McAllister."

Simmons didn't even bother with the niceties. "Do you want the good news or the bad news first?"

"Good news." Was there any other answer?

"We got a hit off the prints from that bag of drugs."

"Thank God for small favors."

The pregnant pause at the other end of the line had Finn's stomach flipping uncomfortably.

"Bad news. They're your girl's."

"Excuse me."

"They were a match for Kentucky Rose Blackburn."

10

"WHAT'S WITH THE DUDE and the dog?" Michelle glanced over her shoulder to where Duchess was curled up beside the bull.

Crap, they hadn't talked about their cover story to explain Duchess, just what to say to explain Finn.

"He trains dogs."

Around her the chaos that normally accompanied her mandatory staff meetings ceased. All attention zeroed in on her, which usually wouldn't have been an issue. Today, it made her want to squirm.

"Oh, like service animals?" Heather asked.

"Something like that," Tucker muttered. She hated lying to her team. "Duchess goes with him everywhere."

Kayla sighed and slumped into her chair. "That's sweet."

She didn't want to admit it, but yeah, the way he was with Duchess was kinda sweet.

"Tucker." Finn's sharp voice cut across the room, contradicting the thought she'd just had.

She held up a hand in his direction, giving him the sign to wait for a second. Everyone's attention had turned from her, and Marcy had just started telling them about her mom's stint in the hospital. She'd been out for a week dealing with that and Tucker wanted to know how things were going.

That was another reason for staff meetings—for everyone to bond and socialize.

"No," a rough voice growled in her ear. "Not in a minute. Now."

He swept a quick, brittle smile around the group. "Sorry, ladies, I need to borrow her for a bit." His words were an apology, but his tone was a command.

Which pissed Tucker off.

"Whatever you need can wa—"

Her words clogged in her throat when she turned. One good look at the thunderous expression on Finn's face and her heart stumbled inside her chest. His deep green eyes were shooting straight into her, blazing with anger.

In that split second she realized she'd never seen him truly livid. Sure, he'd been irritated in the middle of that fight. And she sometimes rubbed him the wrong way, but he seemed to think even that was cute. Staring up at him, she could imagine the men and women he'd caught with illegal drugs cowering before him.

Because as strong as she was, she had to fight that urge herself. Not because she was scared—everything inside her knew Finn would never physically hurt her—but because whatever had upset him wasn't going to be good.

"Now, Tucker. I need to talk to you now."

"Monique, could you take over, please?" she said, not even bothering to turn around to face her team. "I'm sorry, everyone. I'll be back in just a few."

"I wouldn't count on it," Finn growled beneath his breath.

Shaking his grip off, Tucker put some space between them.

He didn't seem to care, just made a curt movement with his hand obviously issuing Duchess a command to stay. He stalked across the bar, and headed down the back hallway and into her tiny office. Holding the door open for her to enter, he slammed it shut with a resounding bang and then flipped the lock for good measure.

"What's going on, Finn?"

"I can't believe I bought it." He stalked forward, shrinking the space between them. His entire body was rock solid, every muscle tense and tight. Not a good sign.

"Bought what?" Tucker instinctively countered with several steps backward. Until her butt hit the edge of her desk and she had nowhere to go.

"The innocent, businesswoman facade. The *I'd never let drugs into my bar* line. The bullshit way you trembled when we found the door to your house open, although maybe that part was real. What happened? Your supplier get pissed that you lost his drugs and come looking for payment? Was that a friendly warning?"

Tucker's legs collapsed, her body folding onto the top of the desk. She stared up at Finn, horror spinning through her.

Had he somehow found out about the drugs she'd discovered? She'd omitted all footage from the one camera that had shown her tumble during the fight—and a small baggie falling out of her pocket—before she'd passed the recording on to Dade and Simmons.

It was obvious he was thinking the worst.

She had to explain. Sweeping her tongue across dry lips, Tucker started to open her mouth.

"Don't even bother," he said in disgust. "I can see the guilt all over your face."

Of course he could. She felt guilty as hell. But that wasn't right, because she hadn't done anything wrong, dammit!

He spun away from her, his body quivering with emotion. "I had my suspicions at first."

Wait. "What?"

"We were told the dealer was a woman. You're perfectly positioned to run that kind of business with the bar as your cover. Of course I suspected you."

Jesus. The entire time he was seducing her, tempting her, kissing the hell out of her… Had he still believed she was involved when they'd slept together?

Just the thought had her own anger roiling.

"But I let my damn dick convince me you couldn't be involved. Hell." He raked his hands through his hair, pulling at the strands. "That was a genius move last night, pushing me away and then coming to my bed."

Okay, now she was downright pissed. She definitely hadn't done anything wrong. But there was a part of her that had always feared Finn wouldn't believe her.

The real issue was—why did it matter?

Before last night Finn wasn't anything to her. Not really. His opinion shouldn't have registered as important.

But it was.

She didn't want him to think the worst of her.

And he damn well owed her the chance to explain.

"I don't know what you think you know, but you're dead wrong."

"Oh, am I?" His voice was silky smooth and deadly.

He stalked forward, crowding into her personal space and looming over her. As much as she hated the reaction, she couldn't stop herself from leaning back, from searching for relief from the intensity that pulsed off him in waves.

What was wrong with her that the energy arching between them had her thighs trembling and her blood pulsing quickly through her veins?

Wrapping both hands around the edge of the desk and bracketing her in, he leaned close. "Why don't you explain to me how your fingerprints ended up on that bag of meth, Kentucky? Explain to me—how could you look yourself in the mirror every morning and sell that poison?"

Tucker couldn't breathe. Finn's gaze bored into her. Anger and anguish filled him up, pouring out through his deep green eyes.

A pit opened up in Tucker's belly. She didn't want to care. Didn't want his pain to matter.

But it did.

"Explain it to me," he snarled, almost begged. "Make me understand how you could sell such an awful, destructive drug? The same drug that stole my sister from me?"

Her mouth opened and closed. Words she wanted to say—needed to say—froze in her throat.

Frustrated, Finn spun away. His fist punched through the wall, leaving a gaping hole. It should have bothered Tucker. It did. But not nearly as much as the sheen of barely checked emotion he was fighting to control.

Finn's display of temper scared her, although probably not the way it should have. She didn't worry about him turning those fists in her direction. Even after only a couple of days she knew him well enough to realize he'd never strike a woman in anger. Nope, it was the overwhelming urge to soothe him that was really dangerous.

He walked around with such confidence and swagger, refusing to apologize for who he was or what he thought. He asked no one for permission or absolution, and that was something she could respect. Even if it drove her batty on occasion. Because she approached life the same way.

Take her or leave her, she wasn't about to change who she was for anyone, let alone a man.

But this…that glimpse of his vulnerability and pain cut straight through to the heart of her. That hole he'd just punched had breached more than the wall. It had busted through just about all of her defenses.

Although that didn't stop her from being angry with him.

"Are you done? Ready to listen to me now?"

Finn glared, shaking his hand even as he didn't seem to want to admit it hurt. "I don't know. Are you going to spout off a bunch of lies?"

"No, but you have no reason to believe me. Because I stupidly didn't tell you at the time, but I actually found those drugs in the bathroom Friday night."

Finn's gaze narrowed.

"Stuffed behind one of the fancy towel holders I have on the counter. I was trying to decide what to do with it when Wyatt called for me. I jammed the baggie into my pocket and ran out. In the melee, I honestly forgot all about it until later."

"Me finding them on the floor didn't jog your memory?"

"No. I had no reason to think the bag I'd found had fallen out. Besides, I'd just gotten my bell rung. My jaw and head were aching. My ankle was throbbing. I wasn't exactly thinking clearly."

The muscle at the edge of his jaw ticked for several interminable seconds before he asked, "Why didn't you tell me all this on Saturday?"

"Because I was pissed at you for maneuvering yourself into my life and my bar. I didn't want you here, Finn. And I didn't think you'd believe me at that point if I tried to tell you the truth."

"You didn't give me a chance to believe you. And now, I'm not sure I can."

Tucker shrugged. What else could she do? She'd given him the truth and the rest was his decision.

"You can have the video footage I didn't include in the DVD I gave to Dade and Simmons."

"Jesus, Tucker," Finn groaned, rubbing his hands over his face. "Withholding evidence like that just makes you look even more guilty."

He wasn't wrong, but there was nothing she could do about it now.

"The footage shows the drugs falling out of my pocket during the fight, Finn. What was I supposed to do? I don't have cameras in the restroom so there's no evidence proving I found them there. I can show you the tape where I dashed out of the ladies', but that's all I've got to back up the story I just told you."

Finn sagged against the wall, letting his body bow inward, running his fingers through his dark brown hair.

"You realize Dade and Simmons are working to build a case against you now."

"They're going to waste their time and miss the real dealer."

She wanted to ask if he believed her, but checked herself just in time. Maybe she didn't really want to know the answer to that right now.

"Well, one thing is for sure. If you're not involved—" he cut her a glance that clearly conveyed exactly what she'd feared, that he wasn't convinced "—then one of your waitresses most likely is."

"What do you mean?"

"You said the drugs were stuffed behind a paper towel holder. No random patron dealing at the bar would leave their stash like that. They'd keep it on them so they could sell more easily. But someone working, that's another story. Maybe she's afraid you, Wyatt or one of the bouncers might catch her with it. She's familiar enough with the building and possible hiding places. She knows where the surveillance cameras are so she can avoid them. Maybe she sells to women in the restroom and men somewhere else."

"Why does it have to be a woman?"

"Because that's the one thing my informant is certain of. And because you claim you found the drugs in the women's restroom."

Tucker sighed and dropped her chin to her chest. This whole situation weighed on her. She was so tired, but she didn't have the luxury of giving into the exhaustion.

This was what she'd been afraid of for the past two days. That restless sense of doom that had been lurking in the back of her brain ever since Finn had walked into her bar with two officers in tow.

Last night had spooked her. She'd already called a friend—a PI who was going to loan her a couple of hidden cameras to set up in some of the areas where she didn't already have surveillance.

In the meantime, maybe she should let Finn question everyone. Being impartial, he'd probably get further than she would. But then, whoever was behind this would know they were on to them.

"Maybe," she agreed reluctantly.

Shaking his head, Finn pushed away from the wall. "I'm going to figure out who's responsible for bringing these drugs into your bar. And I'm going to stop them. No matter what."

He paused for several seconds, those green eyes scoring straight into her, leaving her breathless. "Even if that person is you."

GOD, HE DIDN'T know what to think. Was he being swayed by his attraction for her? His driving need to have and hold her? His desire to discover all the tiny pieces that she worked so hard to keep to herself?

Maybe.

Probably.

But he wasn't sure that made her guilty.

What bothered him most was that his indecisiveness was unnatural, but didn't seem to affect the way he wanted her at all.

He'd spent years fighting the war on drugs. It was his passion in life. If he prevented even one person from dying as Bethany had then it was all worthwhile.

But that mentality came with a clear-cut idea of who the enemy was.

If Tucker was involved, he wasn't sure he'd be able to see her as the enemy. He was already making excuses and rationalizations in his head. Because he believed her when she said she didn't want drugs at her bar. Maybe she'd been coerced? Maybe somehow gotten involved with the wrong people and couldn't find her way out?

He wanted there to be an explanation. And that could be a problem. Because if she was involved it was more likely because she wanted the money—and that would mean she wasn't the woman he thought she was.

For the moment, Finn had decided to believe her. Or at least to keep a muzzle over the tiny voice in the back of his head that kept saying he was being an idiot.

The best thing for him to do was continue on the path they'd started. Eventually, he'd either be proven right or wrong. But the uncomfortable churning in his belly that wouldn't quit was going to be hell to live with in the meantime.

If he'd expected a Sunday night to be the slow part of the weekend, he was wrong. The crowd was a little different, more older couples than searching singles, but the place was still packed, with at least twenty TVs blasting different options from sports to that show about zombies everyone seemed enamored with.

The stage was quiet and the music piped in from the speakers a little lower. Lights didn't flash incessantly over the dance floor, but were a constant muted play of shadow and light. The bull sat silent off to the side, getting a rest of his own.

Finn was impressed that Tucker managed to completely change the feel of the bar based on the clientele that came in. That was a brilliant marketing strategy. Adaptability was one reason she'd found success.

But maybe that was also how she'd gotten involved with meth dealers. Assuming she had. Dammit. Nope, he wasn't going to question this anymore tonight.

Finn slid onto his favorite stool. Duchess plopped down onto the floor at his feet. Her every watchful gaze swept across the room, but she didn't twitch.

Monique was behind the bar tonight. He flashed her a smile and ordered a beer when she got close. She moved efficiently, pouring his drink while taking another order and chatting up a couple.

Finn could see why Tucker kept her around. She was fast and efficient. Friendly, but still managing to give off a *don't mess with me* vibe that no doubt came in handy when things got rowdy.

She delivered his beer, plopping the glass down in front of him. "Thanks," he said, trying to pass her a twenty. She just waved him away.

"Tucker said not to take your money."

Glancing around, Finn tried to find Tucker's cloud of blond hair in the crowd, but couldn't. "Where is she?"

"In the back, talking to one of our suppliers."

"On a Sunday?"

She shrugged. "We had a major problem with our shipment yesterday. She called and reamed him a new one. He dropped everything to hightail it over and smooth her ruffled feathers."

She hadn't said anything to him about a screwed-up delivery. Although, would she? No matter that it felt like they'd known each other forever, their whirlwind relationship had only been going for a few days.

The problem was, he wanted her to. He wanted to be the person she complained to when things went wrong. Her release valve and her sounding board. He wanted to share in her triumphs and the little irritations.

He wanted everything from her.

But right now, he wasn't willing to give her the same.

Because he couldn't. There was a piece of him that just…didn't know. Couldn't quite trust.

Pushing up from the stool, Finn left his beer sitting on the bar. "Don't let anyone spike that, would you?" he asked as he walked away.

Monique chuckled, but grabbed his beer and put it behind the bar.

Weaving through the crowd, he nodded to Matt, one of Tucker's bouncers, from across the room and pointed to the back. He hadn't seen Wyatt since their staff meeting earlier in the day. Maybe it was the guy's night off? Matt returned the nod and waved him through.

Duchess was beside him, right on his hip. This morning he might have promised Tucker that the dog wouldn't go into the back of the bar, but considering the fingerprints they'd discovered today, he was reneging on the agreement.

And didn't feel a single twinge of remorse.

The noise might be muted tonight, but the Rose was still a bar. He much preferred the dark quiet he always found behind the scenes. It was definitely more his speed. Cooler without all the people.

Finn stopped just outside Tucker's office. The door was open an inch or two, so he didn't bother to knock before pushing it in. But a quick sweep of the small space told him the room was empty. Not that he'd necessarily needed to see. He could feel she wasn't there.

With a frown tugging at his lips, Finn systematically checked each of the rooms on his way down the hall. The large area where she kept the liquor stocked. A small storeroom for other supplies. The kitchen where everything was dark because they'd stopped serving food an hour ago.

At the end of the hallway the only door he had left was the one that led out to the back parking lot. It was propped open, which wasn't necessarily unusual. The door had an automatic lock for security reasons, but a couple of Tucker's employees liked to go outside to smoke on their breaks.

The door creaked as he pushed it open, the sound loud in the silent night.

A single light shone over the door, casting a wide circle of yellow onto the dark pavement. The night was chilly, but he didn't care.

Stepping out of the light, Finn set his hand atop Duchess's head and waited for his eyes to adjust to the darkness.

And spotted her almost immediately.

Moonlight rained down over her blond hair, turning it silvery pale. She was facing away from the door with her head tipped back and her arms crossed over her chest.

At first he thought she was staring up at the sky, until he realized her eyes were closed.

Finn started to take a step forward, but motion off to his right stalled him. He turned just in time to catch a man weaving through the cars at the edge of the parking lot that all the employees used.

An engine revved. Headlights beamed on, cutting through the darkness and illuminating the man for a split second before he slipped inside the car.

Finn only caught a glimpse, but it was long enough for him to recognize the man as one of the lieutenants of a local drug kingpin.

There was no good reason for him to be at the Rose. With Tucker outside.

Swallowing hard, Finn let his gaze swing back to Tucker. A heavy band constricted his chest. He didn't want to ask the question, but he had to.

Finn closed the distance between them. "What are you doing out here?"

He kept his voice quiet, in deference to the stillness around them. But he half expected Tucker to startle anyway. She didn't. Instead, she turned her head to him, the ghost of her normally bright smile playing across her lips.

She looked tired.

"I walked one of our distributors out and stayed for a few minutes because I needed a sanity break. It's been a long couple of days."

Yeah, he bet. The only distributor Finn had seen leaving was a drug dealer who was most likely looking for reparation on the product that had been lost.

Dammit. What was wrong with him that he wanted to believe that, if she was up to her eyeballs in this mess, her involvement was involuntary?

Cupping her face in both of his hands, Finn turned her so that she couldn't avoid looking straight at him. He searched her eyes, looking for some sign of guilt or subterfuge. Something that would make this a hell of a lot easier than it was right now.

The clear, steady gaze staring back at him only made things more confusing. She didn't look like she was hiding anything. Was he jumping to conclusions here? He hadn't actually seen the guy anywhere near her. He could just as easily have been here to see someone else—the real dealer.

But he had to ask. "You know I'm here for you, right? Let me help you."

Tucker reached for him, wrapping her fingers around his wrists. At first he wasn't sure if she was holding onto him or about to push him away. Maybe she didn't know, either. But she did neither. She simply stood in his hold.

"I'm fine. Tired and irritated. This isn't the first problem we've had with this distributor, but at least he got his butt in gear and is fixing the error. I'll have what I need by tomorrow afternoon. Although that means on the one day a week I have off I'll have to come here to meet the delivery truck."

Her grip on him tightened and a self-deprecating laugh rolled through her chest. "Who am I kidding? I'd have been here on my day off anyway. I've been here every day since I opened the place."

Staring up at him, her deep blue eyes glittered in the moonlight. "I didn't realize just how lonely and predictable my life had become until you barreled into it, you know? I'm always here because the Rose is all I have. And I'm not sure how to change that. If I *want* to change that. But you're the first person in a long time that's even got me questioning the status quo."

Sonofabitch. Her words punched straight through his gut. Because he wanted that. He wanted *her*. He stared into her gaze, clear and open. Honest.

He felt like he was being torn in two. But right now, despite everything, the side that wanted her was winning over the tiny voice in his brain telling him to proceed with caution. Was that stupidity or instinct? He'd been around long enough to know to trust his gut. And something inside him wanted to believe her.

Dipping down, Finn pressed his mouth to hers. The kiss was nothing like what he'd become used to with her—hot and incendiary. It was easy and soft. Soothing, although the burn of need was still there. It was simply muted, banked.

She clung to him in a way that made him want to scoop her up, press her against his chest and protect her from every damn thing in this world that could hurt her—including herself.

It was obvious she'd been hurt before. By people who were supposed to matter. By people she was supposed to trust.

He didn't want to be another in a long line to disappoint her. But he didn't want to find himself in that situation, either.

The push and pull was killing him, and tonight there was no hope for a solution.

11

It was late, and she was numb with fatigue. Yet Tucker's body buzzed with an energy she couldn't suppress. It had been there since Finn had found her outside and they'd shared that kiss.

He hadn't taken it further, even though she'd wanted him to. He'd brushed his mouth over hers, tasting, savoring, softly tempting. And then he'd set her away from him, killing the moment by pointing her at the door, swatting her ass and telling her to get inside and finish up so they could go home.

She should have been irritated. But she wasn't. Because being irritated over something so silly seemed a pointless waste of time. He was being playful.

By the end of the night, Tucker was dragging. That wasn't unusual for a Sunday. But she really needed that Monday off to recover. And while she usually spent some of the day working anyway, it wasn't the same hectic pace or late night hours.

Once again, Finn waited patiently while she closed up the bar and then ushered her out to his Jeep.

At some point the sneaky bastard had colluded with

Matt to have one of the guys take the car she'd left here last night back to her place, effectively cutting off any argument she might make for going home alone.

Not that she'd particularly wanted to tonight. But it pissed her off that he'd taken the choice away. Not to mention that he'd simply exchanged one argument for another. Though he didn't seem to care. He'd stood, arms crossed over his chest, with an indulgent smile curling those damn lush lips as she'd cursed him.

His lack of engagement had been irritating and less than cathartic. She needed an outlet for the restless energy buzzing beneath her skin, and he wasn't giving it to her.

Duchess bounded up into the Jeep, curling up on the backseat behind her.

She was so calm and quiet. Surprisingly enough, no one had complained about the dog because most patrons seemed oblivious she was even there.

Although, throughout the night Tucker had watched several times as people—mostly women, which she refused to let bother her—approached Finn before crouching down to pet Duchess.

Twisting in her seat, Tucker reached out and scratched Duchess's head. The dog's ears perked up and she nuzzled into Tucker's palm. She was actually getting used to the dog being their silent shadow.

Tucker was so distracted with her thoughts that it took her at least fifteen minutes before she realized they weren't headed in the direction of her place.

"Where are we going? I'm really not up for breakfast again tonight, Finn. I'm tired. It's been a long week. I just want to go to bed."

Her brain said *alone*, but her body thought having Finn next to her was the better option. Since they couldn't seem to agree, she decided to keep her mouth shut and not voice either.

Reaching over, Finn placed his hand on her thigh and squeezed. "Right there with you."

She waited but he didn't elaborate. "So...where are we going?"

"My place."

His place. "Maybe I don't want to go to your place."

Stopping at a red light, he twisted his head to look at her. "I'd love for you to stay at my place tonight, Tucker. But if you'd rather go to your place I'll just grab a few things and we can head that way next. It's up to you." Sweeping his thumb across her cheekbone, he threaded his fingers through the hair at her nape and dipped closer.

Out of the corner of her eye, Tucker saw the light change, but Finn didn't move. He didn't care. The conversation they were having was more important.

The way he was looking at her right now made her feel special. Something akin to hope bloomed deep in her chest, right alongside a spreading ribbon of doubt.

He was too good to be true. This couldn't last. Nothing ever did. But the more time she spent with him the more difficult it became to protect herself from the inevitable pain she knew would eventually come.

"You've had a rough couple days. I thought maybe you wouldn't want to stay at your place. And I know, even if the thought crossed your mind, you probably wouldn't voice it. Or let yourself act on it. Even though you have every right to want some distance for a night or two."

The rhythmic sweep of his thumb across her jaw was

hypnotic. A sense of calm she hadn't even realized she desperately needed seeped through her body.

"You tell me what you want and that's what we'll do."

Damn, he was good.

Clearing her throat, Tucker pulled away. "I suppose it might be nice to stay somewhere else tonight. The house still feels a little…" Her voice trailed off to nothing.

She didn't actually want to say the words. Somehow, saying them felt like giving them power.

"Violated," he murmured in a soft, gruff voice that had a shiver rolling down her spine.

"Yeah," she sighed. That was it exactly. She didn't feel safe there, and that really bothered her. She'd spent a lot of time and money creating the kind of home she'd always wanted growing up. Thinking that getting what she'd spent hours daydreaming about as a kid would solve all of her problems. Would fill the void that seemed to live in the center of her chest.

But with a single, simple act someone had taken that sense of safety and comfort away from her. It hurt, realizing that no matter how hard she'd worked, no home could be perfect or perfectly protected.

And that the void was still there, just waiting for the facade to crumble. She'd done everything right and now look at where she was.

Finn slipped his hand down her neck, across her shoulder and then twined their fingers together. Moving their linked hands to his thigh, he put his attention back on the empty road.

She could feel the solid weight of his muscle flexing as he gave the Jeep more gas. Flutters rioted through her belly. After last night, there was no pretending that they'd be sleeping in separate beds.

And, yes, that kiss out back had pretty much promised that outcome already. And her body was definitely on board. But the reality was hitting her and she was excited and...nervous.

For the rest of the ride, Tucker tried to fight the sensation off. To will it away. But it wasn't going anywhere. Instead, it eased off to a gentle effervescence that felt remarkably like happiness.

To say Finn's place wasn't quite what she'd expected was an understatement. Though, that implied she'd actually spent time contemplating where Finn lived, which, until very recently, she really hadn't.

His house was...modern. With sharp angles and lots of glass. It was open and airy, words she never would have used to describe the man who owned the place.

Thinking about it now, she wouldn't have been surprised by a log cabin or even a loft apartment. Something decidedly bachelor and a little rough around the edges.

While the place clearly had a masculine vibe to it, it was gorgeous in its own stark way.

And that did remind her of Finn. Or the Finn she was coming to know. He was no-nonsense and few frills. Function and form over showy and useless details.

Holding the front door open, he let Duchess inside first. She disappeared into the back of the house, no doubt to find her own bed for the night. She might have been quiet and curled up in a corner most of the evening, but even Tucker recognized the dog had been attentive and watchful the entire time.

Finn led her through to the kitchen, full of black granite and glossy cabinets. The space should have been oppressively dark, but somehow wasn't. Maybe it was the metallic accents, high ceilings and bright moonlight streaming through all the glass.

The space had a sleek and sophisticated edge to it.

"Did you use a decorator?"

The words just blurted out of her mouth. Although she couldn't imagine him discussing paint colors and knickknacks with a perfectly styled consultant, that was easier to swallow than *him* caring about those things.

"No."

Opening a wine fridge built into the center island, Finn pulled out a bottle, grabbed a glass and poured. She thought about refusing when he held it out to her, but a glass actually sounded perfect right now. Maybe it would help her mellow.

"Thanks." Gripping the stem, she took a swallow of the cool, crisp white, letting the flavor of it roll across her tongue. She might run a bar that was better known for its craft beer selection and top-shelf liquor than wine, but that didn't mean she couldn't appreciate a good one when she tasted it.

"Mmm," she said, lifting her glass in appreciation. "Good."

"I know."

"Cocky ass."

His grin widened, crinkling the corners of his eyes in a way that was way too appealing. "Know that, too."

Letting out a sigh, Tucker turned away and started wandering. The entire downstairs was open. On one end was a huge black leather sofa. It looked really comfortable. The kind perfect for burrowing beneath a fluffy blanket and curling up with a good book.

A monstrous TV was mounted on the wall and she

also noticed speakers strategically suspended from the ceiling.

But what really caught her attention were the photographs scattered around the room. They were gorgeous.

Grouped together in clusters, for the most part they seemed to be nature shots. Some in black and gray, others in vivid color. A handful of some stark, rocky mountains that seemed so desolate, and yet so hopeful they made her chest ache. A series of clouds that, put together, told the story of a storm rolling across an open field, ending with a brilliant flash of lightning striking the ground.

"These are gorgeous," she said, twisting around to find Finn standing quietly behind her, hands stuffed in the pockets of his jeans, just watching.

"Thank you."

"Where'd you get them? That storm series would look amazing in the bar."

"If you want copies I'll print them off for you."

"No. Isn't that illegal or something? I'm sure the artist would want to get paid for the work."

"I don't sell my photographs."

His words sank in and slowly Tucker turned. This time, she really took him in when she looked. And recognized the tiny signs of tension she'd missed before because she was so captivated by his art.

"You took these photographs?"

Finn shrugged, looking a little sheepish. The expression was completely unexpected, and therefore all the more endearing.

"It's been a hobby since I was a little kid. My mom was often taking pictures of my sister and I when we were younger. You know, as moms do."

No, she wouldn't know, but now wasn't the time to remind him of that.

"One day she had it out, taking pictures of Bethany while she was doing something or other. I don't remember what. But she put it down and I just picked it up. I like the way the world looks through the tiny window on a camera. Small, but somehow still with infinite possibilities."

She watched his gaze track to the photographs hanging on the wall behind her. The quiet curl of pride on his lips.

"Those photographs remind me of places I've been," he continued. "Things I've experienced. People who matter."

"I don't see any portraits."

"No. I keep those somewhere else. Maybe one day I'll show them to you."

Something told Tucker that, if that ever happened, it would mean something more profound than simply opening a scrapbook. He'd be introducing her to something—someone—important.

"I'd like that."

It felt strange and perfect having her at his place. Watching her reaction to his photographs made his chest tighten in a way that left him itching to relieve the pressure.

He'd had plenty of people over before. Hell, he'd had plenty of *women* over to his place before. But their reaction had never really mattered to him. Definitely not the way Tucker's apparently did.

The urge to sweep her into his arms and devour her mouth was overwhelming and too much for him to ignore.

The kiss was gentle, but his hold on her wasn't. She was so soft and feminine. Fragile, or at least she felt that way in his arms. Moments like these, he was afraid he might hurt her.

Even though he knew Tucker was tougher than that, he couldn't shake the sensation. It made him want to protect her. Treasure her.

And he couldn't find it in him to think that was wrong. Because in his mind, it wasn't. He was very quickly coming to care about this woman, and in his world that meant something very specific. Responsibility.

He was so afraid she was going to slip through his fingers. They butted heads. He craved her like the worst addiction. And there was the very real possibility that she was playing him.

Although he couldn't think about that right now. The possibility certainly didn't stop how much he wanted her.

Her entire body melted, opening, giving.

Grasping her hips, Finn boosted her up until her legs wrapped around his waist. Blindly, he walked forward until her back collided with the wall.

"I need you. Now," he rumbled.

"Yes." Her voice was breathy as her greedy hands plucked at his clothes, trying to find bare skin.

He was too busy searching for more of her to help. They tore at each other's shirts, jeans and underwear. Finn was pretty sure he heard a seam rip, but he had no idea if it was hers or his.

Who cared?

His mouth found the hot velvet of her naked skin, licking and sucking. She tasted like heaven, sweet and salty. This wasn't enough. And she deserved more than to be shoved up against a wall and devoured.

Tucker Blackburn was the kind of woman you savored, every chance you got.

Tightening his hold on her, Finn stumbled down the hallway toward his bedroom. He didn't bother flipping on any lights.

Dropping her to the bed, he loved the way she sprawled out in the middle of his big mattress. "Perfect." She belonged right there.

Gripping her waist, he flipped her over onto her belly.

"Wait. What?" Tucker craned her neck around, trying to scramble onto her knees.

Placing his big hands in the center of her back, Finn gently kept her in place. "Relax."

And then he started kneading her shoulders, digging his fingers into muscles she probably didn't even realize were tight. Within minutes all the tension was leaking from her body. She was practically a puddle in the center of his bed, naked and spread eagled.

Her skin glowed, pale and luminous. So soft and beautiful.

Over and over again, he swept his fingers down the curve of her back. Over her ribs and hips. Along the line of her ass. His touch changed, from relaxing to caressing. From massaging to arousing. And the moan she let out was his reward.

Her hips shifted restlessly against his bed and her legs scissored open in invitation.

Leaning over her, he pressed his wide chest to the slope of her back, murmuring into her ear, "Do you have any idea how gorgeous you are right now? Your skin flushed with wanting me. Those restless little pants you can't quite contain are driving me mad."

Tipping her head back, she found the line of his throat and sucked. Her tongue laved at him, even as he let his weight settle over her, pressing her deeper into the bed.

With one hand, he spread her thighs open wider. The other ran up the soft inside of her leg, until he finally hit home.

God, she was so wet, and the second he touched her, her entire body shuddered. Nestled so close, he could feel every nuance of her reaction.

It was breathtaking and made him feel like the most powerful man on the earth. Because she was so strong and was giving him everything right now.

His erection throbbed with the need to be buried inside her, connected and surrounded by everything about her.

Grasping her hips, Finn pulled her up onto her knees. She knew exactly what he wanted, collapsing forward onto her elbows and giving him the best view of her swollen, drenched sex.

Fishing for a condom in the bedside drawer, he quickly sheathed himself before holding her steady and thrusting deep.

Her fingers twisted in the sheets and a hard gasp escaped her parted lips. Her hips rocked against him, asking for more. Together, they found a rhythm that had stars bursting across his vision.

"So good," she panted out in time with the tempo of his thrusts. She wasn't wrong, but this wasn't enough. Pulling out, he urged Tucker onto her back and hooked his arms beneath her elbows, holding her as he sank deep.

Those beautiful blue eyes glittered up at him, vague

and full of bliss. All the walls she kept in place were gone, down, and he could see everything she probably didn't want him to know.

Everything about this woman called to him. It wasn't just her attitude, intelligence or lithe body. Any of those things could be intriguing, but the whole package is what held him captivated.

Even now, when a part of him realized it would be smart to hold a piece of himself back, he just couldn't.

In that moment, joined with her in a way that was far more than physical, he couldn't seem to stop the tumble.

There was a frenzy, not just in the need for a release he could only find with her, but for more. Her understanding, her support.

Her love.

Because in that moment, he had no doubt that she held every single piece of him in her tiny hands.

The realization was scary and exhilarating.

"Finn," she breathed when he lingered on the edge just a little too long, staring down at her without moving. Her hips bucked up, trying to find the friction that would send her over.

Threading his fingers in her hair, Finn held her steady so he could look straight into her eyes as he began to move. He wasn't about to let her hide. Although, in forcing her to acknowledge the connection between them, he was spilling himself at her feet, as well.

Giving her everything.

Her hands ran over his back and sides, arms and shoulders. Touching any inch of him she could reach. Her touch felt so good, lighting him up and sending energy dancing across his skin.

Leaning down, he found her mouth. His hips pistoned against hers, drowning in the sensation of her. Words fell from him, murmured against her lips and chin and throat. There was no telling what he confessed.

This need for her spiraled out of control, but not before he felt her entire body clamp tight around him. His name was a keening cry muffled by her mouth in the curve of his neck.

She trembled against him, racked by wave after wave of her orgasm. Her release triggered his own, euphoria erupting through every inch of his body, emptying straight into Tucker. And he'd never felt more powerful in his life, even as his arms wrapped tight around her, sheltering her through that storm.

Together, they collapsed onto the bed. Finn maneuvered them both until he could pull the covers over their sweat-slicked skin. He didn't want her to get cold.

Her body boneless, Tucker let him. And almost as amazing as the orgasm he'd just experienced was the bliss when she curled up against him, her mouth nuzzling sleepily against his throat and shoulder.

His arm tightened around her, wanting to keep her there, next to him, forever.

12

It was dark when Tucker's eyes opened. For a few seconds she was disoriented, unsure exactly where she was. The room wasn't hers.

In a blinding rush, the entire night crashed over her.

Her fight with Finn. Seeing his house and getting a glimpse into the man he didn't let many people see.

The sex. Unbelievable, soul-stirring, life-altering sex.

Her chest tightened and the need to run overwhelmed her. Suddenly, the room felt like it was closing in on her. He'd made her feel. The memory of emotions she didn't want sent panic rolling faster through her belly.

Damn him for pushing her to that point and leaving her protective layers in tatters between them.

Rolling over, she intended to get up and...what? Walk home? Call a cab?

Tucker had no idea, but she couldn't stay in his bed.

Her feet hadn't even hit the floor before a low, lazy voice asked, "Going somewhere?"

Her gaze flew to the dark corner of the room where Finn sat in a chair. Moonlight fell across him, illuminating half of his face and leaving the rest of it in cloaking shadows.

"No." Bullshit. She wasn't going to lie to him. "Yes. What are you doing lurking in the dark? That's not creepy or anything."

His lips quirked up at one corner. "I couldn't sleep. Didn't want to leave you alone in a strange place after the last couple days. You know running isn't going to change anything, right?"

God, how could this man know her so damn well after just a few days?

"Not to mention that I'll just have to go after you."

"Isn't that called stalking?" she sneered, lashing out because the deeper she got with Finn the more she felt like she was drowning with no savior in sight.

His eyes narrowed, but the smirk on his face didn't budge. "Kitten, you tell me right now that you don't feel what's building between us and I'll let you walk out the door without another word. There's a difference between choosing to walk away from someone and running because you're scared of what they make you feel. So, say it."

Tucker swallowed. The words welled up. She wanted to let them out, to free herself from this whole mess and from the jumbled, uncomfortable, scary things that Finn created inside her.

But they wouldn't come.

Instead, she watched Finn unfold from the chair. For the first time she realized he was completely naked. God, he was beautiful. The pulse and flow of his body. Powerful and graceful. Those wide shoulders that were perfect for cradling her head. The riot of colorful ink down both of his arms and across his chest. The way he moved, always with direction and purpose.

That was what excited her. He was intent and aware, not just of her, but of everything.

Learning about his photography had surprised her... for about sixty seconds, until she really thought about it. Wasn't that just an extension of who and what he already was?

Finn watched the world. Often, especially at her bar, he was a silent observer, letting the chaos and the noise swirl unheeded around him while he concentrated on more important things. His photographs simply allowed everyone else to get a glimpse of what he saw.

Crossing to the bed, he pressed a knee to the mattress, dipping it beneath her. His hand cupped her neck, drawing her up until his mouth pressed softly against hers.

The kiss was...everything. Passion and comfort, praise and promise.

Pulling back, those green eyes stared straight into her. "If you think you're the only one who finds this unsettling and intimidating, then you're wrong. You make me feel things, Tucker. Things I'd have an easier time not feeling. But that's not how life works."

What was she supposed to say to that?

When he took a step backward, for the first time Tucker realized Finn was cradling an expensive camera in his hand.

"What are you doing?" she asked. "Were you taking pictures of me as I slept? Naked?"

She wasn't sure whether she should be pissed or aroused. Or both. A part of her was affronted that he hadn't bothered asking her. But when did he ever? And having seen his work, it was flattering to think that he'd wanted to capture images of her to keep.

"Chill out. You were covered. I wouldn't cross that line unless you agreed," he said, raising a single eyebrow.

That hellish, beautiful ache he could stir between her thighs with nothing more than a glance was back, greedy and insistent.

"Here," Sitting on the bed beside her, Finn turned the camera so that she could see the small screen across the back.

Pictures of her filled the space. Slowly, he scrolled through thirty or forty of them.

"These are...amazing." Although, just like everything else so far with Finn, they made her feel conflicted. There was something about them that made her look...vulnerable. And she didn't like to think of herself that way.

Maybe it was because she was asleep. Oblivious. Her mouth was slightly open, head resting on an arm and her body curled around one of his pillows. Light and shadow played over her face, making her look younger than she actually was.

She looked innocent, something she hadn't felt since her early teenage years.

"You're always gorgeous, Tucker. But I have to admit, when I woke up and saw you like this I knew I needed to capture the moment. You looked so comfortable and relaxed in my bed. I wanted to remember that you could be this way instead of the intense, independent, stubborn woman I've been butting my head against for days."

Tucker didn't know what to do with that. It irritated

her, but she couldn't deny he was right. There was something about Finn that made her feel centered and easy. No one had ever done that for her, not even her dad. Yes, her father loved her and would do anything for her, but constantly worrying about him had been a major source of restlessness growing up.

She didn't want to think too deeply about that, though. Not right now.

Grabbing the camera, she took it from his hands and turned the lens on him.

"Fair is fair," she said, before clicking the button to record an image of him on the screen.

It was terrible—especially in comparison with the photographs he'd taken—slightly blurry, with half of his body cut out of the frame. But it made Tucker laugh.

Scooting back on the bed, she moved farther away so she could get a better shot and tried again. At least this time he was clear, although his hands were half in front of his face, reaching out. "Give that back, Tucker. It's expensive."

"And I promise not to break it. Now put your hands down."

His mouth twisted into a grimace, but he did as she asked. However, he turned away from her, giving her his profile instead. And looking through the viewfinder, she realized he was uncomfortable.

"You don't like having your picture taken." It was so unexpected, Tucker blurted it out without thinking.

Finn looked at her from the corner of his eye. "No, not really."

Oooh, she could torture him with this, sorta like he tortured her with that damn nickname he insisted on using.

Rising onto her knees, Tucker brought the camera to her eye and started snapping one picture after another. She pressed closer, getting right into his face so he couldn't avoid her, zooming in on his rueful expression.

But that didn't last long. Plucking her up, Finn dropped her back onto the bed and snatched the camera from her hands.

"Hey!"

"You realize two can play that game, right, kitten?"

Finn fiddled with the camera, messing with some of the complicated dials and buttons on the back.

"Why do you insist on calling me that when you know it drives me crazy?"

Although, she had to admit, she was getting used to it. When he first started using the name it irritated the hell out of her. Now…she wouldn't admit this to him without torture, but it made her feel special.

"*Because* it drives you crazy."

"And that's entertaining?"

He glanced up from what he was doing, "Sure. But it's more than that. From the first moment I met you, you reminded me of a feral alley cat."

"Gee, thanks."

"Relax, kitten. I mean it as a compliment. Alley cats are strong."

"Dirty, covered in muck and stinky."

He shrugged. "They have their scars, but so do you. You're gorgeous anyway."

He leaned close, nuzzling her neck. "Smell pretty good, too," he said, before nipping at the pulse just below her ear.

Tucker squealed and attempted to curl her body into a protective ball. But with him lodged between her thighs, the best she could do was wrap herself around him. He sucked and nibbled at her skin. His fingers raced, tickling and then teasing until she was panting from laughter and the exertion of trying to protect herself from his torture.

Finn stepped back. Tucker collapsed onto the bed, arms flung, legs spread, lungs heaving, not caring that she was completely naked until Finn brought the camera to his face and pressed the button that engaged the shutter.

Piling her hands one over the other, she shoved them at the business end of the lens. "What the hell! You said no naked pictures unless I agreed."

From behind the heavy piece of equipment, she could just make out the edge of his grin. "I just got your face, kitten. Promise. Couldn't resist your flushed skin and the remnants of laughter in your eyes."

FINN SNAGGED HER wrists and pulled them out of the way.

Her eyes closed tight against the burst of flash and before she could open them again Finn's mouth found hers. He devoured her, thrusting his tongue between her parted lips. An arm snaking around her body, he held her close even as he kept pressing the button, grabbing shot after shot. No doubt most of them were crooked or cut off.

But neither of them seemed to care.

Disengaging, Finn gently pushed her back against the bed and held up the camera. This time, the quirk of his eyebrow silently asked her for permission.

"If these end up on the internet I'm going to hunt you down and hurt you," was her only answer.

"I don't share, so no worries about that. These are just for me."

He began posing her, rolling her to her belly so that he could take a shot of the curve of her shoulder and back. Asking her to look at him, catching a glimpse of her face surrounded by the cloud of her messy curls. Capturing his strong, rough hand resting on the slope of her pale thigh.

When he asked, she'd expected he'd want something a little more…risqué. But slowly, after about twenty minutes, Tucker realized he was actually fascinated with the lines of her body and how they came together to form the whole.

And somewhere in the middle of the experience, she relaxed and accepted the way he saw her—perfect just as she was.

Shortly after that, Finn abandoned the camera, placing it on the nightstand. He loved her, gently, completely, consuming every inch of her in a way that left her breathless and dizzy.

And this time, when she curled up beside him, none of the apprehension and fear remained. All that was left was a quiet acceptance that this was happening.

Despite everything, she was falling for this man. It might be fast and there were times when he drove her mad. But that didn't matter.

Finn McAllister was a good man, who, she was slowly beginning to hope, wouldn't hurt or leave her.

THE LAST FEW days had been quiet and unproductive. At least as far as the case was concerned. Nothing had happened. Despite being at the bar a little bit each day, Duchess hadn't found anything suspicious.

That should have made Finn feel better. Instead, it was setting him on edge, making everything worse.

The longer he spent with Tucker, the deeper entwined with her he was becoming. Each day he fell a little harder, and almost in direct correlation, the tension inside him grew greater and greater.

He was just waiting for it to explode all around him.

The lab had confirmed the drugs he found at the Rose carried the same chemical signature as the others they'd confiscated, including those from Sergeant Freeman.

Something had to give. Soon. Finn was walking a razor's edge, and the longer it took, the more difficult it became to stay rational and impartial.

"You're sure you've searched every room in the bar?" Dade's voice crackled into the cell phone. "We're missing something here, McAllister."

Which really meant the cop thought *he* was missing something. And that rankled.

"Duchess and I have been here for days. She's one of the best in her field. Trust me, she'd have been able to scent the slightest trace of drugs on anyone in the bar."

Unfortunately, the voice inside his head was screaming terrible things—like the reason they hadn't found anything else was because the dealer had been tipped off. Although, as far as he was aware, Tucker was the only person who knew his ulterior motives for hanging around the Rose—even if those lines had long since blurred.

Where Tucker was concerned, he was a jumbled-up mess. He wanted to believe in her innocence, but couldn't quite pull it off. Partly because it felt like Bethany all over again. He didn't want to turn a blind eye to a problem if it was staring him in the face.

At least he hadn't seen any evidence of Tucker using.

And they'd been spending enough time together that he would have noticed.

Although he wasn't certain that made it better. Because the alternative was that she was potentially just a dealer, pushing drugs that killed other people for the sole purpose of monetary gain.

And while he knew she had her vices—the expensive heels came to mind—so far she hadn't struck him as overly concerned with amassing material things.

What he did know was that she loved her bar. Had invested not just her heart, but her self-worth in the success of the place. Which could be dangerous. Enough to push her into something stupid?

A jumbled mess.

After talking for a few more minutes, Finn hung up with Dade and turned his focus back to the bar.

Tonight, the Rose was as quiet as he'd seen the place. Wednesday nights were apparently a little less chaotic and loud. There were a few regulars, people he recognized because he'd been paying such close attention. But, so far, none of them were raising any red flags.

Since the crowd was lighter, Tucker's staff moved a little slower than normal. The waitresses didn't dance on the bar nearly as often. And several times he noticed them knotted up at the opposite end of the bar, just chatting.

Wyatt and Matt were the only guys in tonight, which made sense since the likelihood of a problem was pretty slim.

Tucker's head of security plopped down onto the stool beside him.

"You've been around a lot lately."

Finn shrugged. "Don't plan on going anywhere as long as Tucker wants me here."

Wyatt grunted, the sound could have meant anything from agreement to concern.

"Slow tonight."

"Wednesdays usually are. I've talked to her about closing a couple more days during the week, but she doesn't like to have the place sitting empty. Something about sunk costs and any sales helping the bottom line."

Now it was his turn to grunt a reply. That definitely sounded like the Tucker he was learning to recognize.

Monday they'd come to the bar and he'd spent a couple of hours watching her deal with paperwork—and meet the distributor with the corrected shipment, which did make him feel a hell of a lot better, at least for a little while.

He'd been amazed at the spreadsheets she'd pored over. When he'd asked, she'd shown him the detailed cost/benefit analysis, not only for each night of the week for the last several months, but on each product they offered in the kitchen.

While he wasn't entirely surprised by her thoroughness, it had impressed him. He'd always known she wasn't some ditzy blonde stumbling her way through running a business. Actually, she reminded him more and more of a captain he'd known over in Afghanistan. A man he greatly admired.

"Honestly." Wyatt leaned forward, crossing his arms over the bar and staring at the wood. "She'd kill me if she knew I was saying anything, but maybe you can talk some sense into her. I'm worried about her. She's working herself to the bone and I don't know how much longer she can last."

Wyatt wasn't saying anything Finn hadn't noticed himself. Tucker worked long hours, late into the night.

She was on her feet most of that time, dragging, serving and lifting, and doing it all with a smile and keen eye toward customer service.

She was always on. Always vigilant.

And when the bar was closed, she was handling paperwork, distributors, accounting and managerial tasks. He didn't need a road map drawn for him to know the Kentucky Rose was everything to her.

"She's sunk every penny she has into this place. Used some money her aunt left her, but that master's was expensive and she spared no expense making this place fabulous. I'm pretty sure she's swimming in debt. Skating on the edge of disaster, man, and I'm really afraid something's eventually going to push her off. Push her to do something desperate."

Wait, what? Everything Tucker had shared with him Monday about the business had made him believe the Rose was profitable. Although, she hadn't actually shown him her bank balances or anything.

The vision of her standing in the middle of a sea of shoes flashed through his mind. Would she buy those things if she couldn't afford them? He'd been joking before about her addiction...but maybe it was real?

He, better than most, realized that people were masters at showing the world exactly what they wanted everyone to see. At hiding the dark and ugly pieces.

Could the information Tucker had shared with him Monday been a misdirection? At the time, her willingness to give him a glimpse into the inner workings of the Rose had meant so much, because he knew how important the bar was to her. Now...

Wyatt shifted uncomfortably, cutting his gaze over to Finn, a deep frown digging grooves around his mouth.

"I know she ran into some unexpected issues renovating this building. Spent more than she'd planned to open the place. And then a couple months ago, the refrigerator busted. Leaked all over, ruined the floor. Both had to be replaced. There's no telling how much that cost her.

"I've spent enough time around bars to know the Rose is doing okay, but she was skating thin already… I'm just worried. And you know she won't let anyone help."

Wyatt's words soured the beer in Finn's belly.

"I didn't tell you this to dump the problem in your lap," Wyatt said, cutting him a somber glance. "I genuinely care about her. And you guys seem to have gotten close awfully fast. Just…keep an eye on her, yeah?"

Pushing away from the bar, Wyatt walked away, leaving Finn's head spinning with unhappy thoughts.

Simmons had pulled financial information on Tucker when they'd decided to use the Rose. Nothing suspicious had come up. But, Finn realized that didn't necessarily mean it wasn't there. It looked like they needed to dig a little deeper.

Maybe Wyatt was lying? But what motive did he have for that?

Finn didn't have any of the answers right now, which only made the restlessness he'd been fighting worse.

But at least there was something he could mark off the list right now.

Dade's earlier question rang through his head. With all the time Duchess had spent at the Rose, there was one room she hadn't actually entered.

Tucker's office.

13

GOD, SHE HAD a headache.

Leaning over, Tucker dropped her head into her hands and dug her fingers into both temples. Squeezing her eyes shut, she willed the pounding pressure to go away. Nothing was helping tonight.

She'd already popped a couple of aspirin and abandoned the floor, which she hated doing even on a slow night. She liked to maintain a presence, not just for her customers but her staff, as well. They needed to know she was there, ready to back them up.

Tonight, she simply couldn't do it. The last several days—and the miniscule amount of sleep she'd been getting thanks to Finn's ability to keep her engine revved—were catching up to her. Stress, pressure, anxiety, excitement.

The door to her office creaked open. She didn't have to look up to know Finn was standing there, so in tune with him after such a short time that she could feel him, her body reacting to his presence on an elemental level. Which was scary as hell in its own right.

"Surprised to find you back here. Everything okay?"

Dropping her head against the raised back of her leather executive chair, Tucker let her eyes open, wincing at the stab of pain caused by the glare from the overhead light.

"Not really. I have a hell of a headache. Already taken something, but it isn't helping."

Duchess slipped into the room behind him just as he closed the door. Walking around to her, Finn rested his hips against the edge of her desk. She stared up at him, unable to tamp down the thrill that shot through her body whenever he was close. He placed his wide, warm palms on either side of her head.

"I'm sorry," he murmured, digging his fingers right into the spot she'd been trying to massage a few minutes ago. With much better results than she'd been getting.

After several quiet moments, the tension in her scalp eased, a melting sensation slipping down her neck and shoulders, arms and chest.

Tucker let out a pent-up breath of relief.

The pain ratcheted down to a dull ache that was manageable. And as her discomfort faded, her awareness of him grew. The solid heat of his thigh pressed against her own leg. The way he loomed over her, taking up all the space.

He'd touched her numerous times, but not quite like this, unbelievably soothing and soft. Still, tonight for the first time she'd noticed just how large his hands were. How capable and strong.

The kind a woman could get used to depending on.

"You're running yourself ragged, Tucker. You need to take it easy. The Rose won't collapse without you for a few hours or, God forbid, an entire night."

She knew he was right, but she just couldn't seem

to let loose of the reins. "I've poured everything I have into this place."

His fingers stilled for several seconds before resuming their slow, rhythmic cadence across her skin.

"But taking a break only ensures you have more to pour back into it later. Why are you so driven? It isn't healthy. Or normal, Tucker."

She laughed, the sound carrying a rough edge to it. "Hello pot, meet kettle."

Finn shook his head. "I know where my focus comes from, but I also recognize that balance is important."

"Sure. What have you done for the last few days outside of this case?"

His fingers slipped from her temples, ghosting over her throat and sending a shiver that rocked through her body.

"I have other reasons for being here, Tucker. Just as important to me as this case. And you haven't answered my question. Why the Rose? Why a bar? You have an MBA. You're intelligent and dynamic. You could do anything you wanted."

"Are you calling my life's goal unworthy?"

"Not a chance. I value my life too much." Finn chuckled, the sound warm and rich. It melted over her, like the best chocolate. She wanted to hear it again and again, mostly because she realized it was rare.

For someone who was calling her on closing herself off, Finn certainly had the same tendencies. She'd watched him over the last week, surrounded by a roomful of people—with plenty of women eyeing him—but he ignored them all.

He was content with the stool against the wall at the

end of her bar. He liked to observe, process, take everything in.

"And, no, there's nothing wrong with owning a bar. I've watched you and you're amazing at running this place. It's clear this isn't just a job for you, but a passion."

"So what's your problem?"

"I worry about how you'd handle it if something happened to this place. How far would you go to keep it running?"

That was an easy question to answer. "I'd do just about anything."

His fingers, stroking softly across her skin, stilled. For several strong heartbeats, his gaze drilled into hers. She fought against the innate need to look away, protect herself. It was a little late for that.

"That's what I'm afraid of," he finally said, the words soft and low.

She didn't understand what he meant, but something told her the statement went much deeper than it appeared. "What's that supposed to mean?"

"Nothing."

"Don't pull that bullshit. You didn't mean nothing."

Finn's lips parted. But before he could say what he was thinking, Duchess's loud, deep bark burst through the room.

Tucker jumped. Not only had she forgotten the dog was there, the only time she'd heard her make much of any noise was the night she'd found the drugs beneath the table.

Finn, however, didn't even flinch. Instead, his hands, resting on her shoulders, tightened for several seconds, to the point that Tucker nearly winced. His jaw snapped shut and a hard line bracketed either side of his mouth.

Those deep green eyes, which had the ability to slay her with nothing but a flicker, turned sharp and cold.

Leaning backward, Finn peered at the floor on the other side of her desk.

"Good girl," he murmured, giving a sharp hand signal that had Duchess dropping back into silence as suddenly as the barking had started.

Finn stood. Grasping Tucker's shoulders, he pulled her up with him. Leading her in front of him, he crossed the room to the far wall. Duchess had dropped to the floor, right in front of the built-in safe.

"What's inside there, Tucker?"

"Money, contracts, the mortgage paperwork for the bar and my house. You know, the kind of things most people put inside a safe."

He nodded, his face grim and determined. Harsh.

Tucker swallowed. For some reason the backs of her eyes burned.

"Open it."

It wasn't a question. It was an order. Some instinct made her want to deny him simply because she could and it bothered her that he felt the need to issue edicts. If he'd asked nicely she would have done it without a second thought.

But the expression on his face told her this was not the time to make a stand on principle.

Reaching up to the keypad, she pressed the numbers by memory, not even caring he could be memorizing them. The lock disengaged with a pop. Gripping the handle, she pulled the door open.

And stood there, stunned.

Inside was a gallon-sized plastic bag, rolled up, containing an obscene amount of meth. Beside that were at least twenty small baggies with what were intended to be individual portions. And as if that wasn't bad enough, the two bricks of cash sitting beside the drugs had her eyes bugging out of her head.

"How the hell did that get in there?"

"I don't know, Tucker. You tell me."

She tried to back away, her entire world suddenly feeling so…wrong. Like somewhere in the last hour she'd slipped down Alice's rabbit hole to find herself in an alternate universe.

This couldn't be real.

But there was nowhere for her to go. Her back hit the solid wall of Finn's chest.

She spun around. He let her, but didn't take his hands off her. As if he was afraid she might try to break for the door.

"Dammit, someone broke into my safe."

"And left you drugs and money? I find that hard to believe."

"I don't care what you believe." But she did. Oh, God, she did.

Swallowing hard, Tucker fought down the torrent of words that wanted to gush out. Protestations of her innocence, because she was really afraid they wouldn't matter.

God, the disgust that clouded Finn's gaze cut straight through her. Her chest ached. No, her entire body throbbed with the pain of that expression.

"You've been playing me the entire time, haven't you? Keep your friends close and your enemies closer? The reason we haven't been able to find anything over the last few days was because you were fully aware we were looking. You tried to keep Duchess out of the bar, and then away from back here when you realized that wouldn't work. How long were you going to let it go on, Tucker?"

He finally released her, taking several large steps backward and running his hands through his hair, tugging at the short strands.

"I have to give it to you. If nothing else, you're dedicated. But then, that's just who you are, isn't it? You're the woman who will give absolutely anything to make this place work. Including sleeping with the guy intent on exposing you. Isn't that what you said only a few minutes ago?"

"No. That isn't..." Tucker's voice trailed off. "I didn't mean it that way," she whispered.

"Oh, I know. But only because you thought you were going to get away with it. I'm here to promise that you won't."

IT HURT TO look at her. He was so angry and disappointed. God, how could he have gotten everything so terribly wrong?

Even now, in the face of overwhelming evidence, he couldn't quite kill the hope that Tucker was innocent. But it was difficult to believe in her while staring at a safe full of drugs in her office.

Could she be telling the truth? Could someone have planted them?

As far as he knew, she was the only person aware that he and Duchess were here to catch a drug dealer, and up until right now there'd been no action for days. A little too convenient.

God, he wanted to believe her…but he couldn't. He couldn't allow himself to look past the obvious and let someone else get hurt. Not again.

The expression on Tucker's face, full of agony, cut straight through him. He didn't doubt she truly felt it. But that wasn't going to change what he had to do.

He'd spent his entire adult career fighting to keep meth off the streets and away from people like his sister. It physically hurt to realize the woman he'd fallen in love with was part of the problem.

Pulling his cell out of his pocket, Finn punched in Dade's number.

"What are you doing?" Tucker asked.

Running a hand over his face, Finn positioned himself in front of the door. If Tucker tried to run she'd have to go through him and Duchess first. "Calling Dade to come and pick you up."

"What?" The incredulity in her tone had the anger beating back the disappointment. Had she really expected he'd let his attachment to her sway him from doing the right thing?

"You're dealing drugs, Tucker. What did you expect me to do when I found out?"

"Please listen to me, Finn," she said, grasping for his hand. He just pulled it out of her reach and placed the call on speaker, instead. "Those drugs are not mine."

Even in the face of overwhelming evidence against her, she was still arguing her innocence. And maybe that's what hurt the most. If she'd told him she was sorry. Asked for his help. Admitted what she'd done— and why—he might have been able to deal with it. Help her.

Instead, she stood there, bags of meth practically

spilling out of the open safe behind her, and continued to try and convince him.

"Do you really think I'm that gullible and stupid?"

"Dade."

"Man, you and Simmons need to get over here now. I found a stash of drugs in Tucker's safe. Duchess and I have her confined to the office."

"Those are not my drugs," she said again, her voice low and even. "Dade, you have to believe me."

"On our way," was Dade's only response before the line went dead.

God, this was a complete mess. "Look, Tucker. Call your attorney and have him meet you at the station. It's possible he can get bail set quickly so you'll only be in there a couple hours. Explain to him how you got dragged into this mess and maybe he'll be able to get you a plea deal. Whatever you do, don't lie to the court."

Her eyes flashed, brilliant with anger and pain. "You're not listening to me."

"No, I'm listening. I'm just not buying the lies anymore."

"I. Am. Not. Lying. Those aren't my drugs, Finn, and if you let them charge me with this no one will be looking for the person who's really dealing. The person who evidently set me up."

He watched a whirlwind of emotions flood her face, so tangled up he couldn't have pulled them apart if he'd wanted to. She moved restlessly, pacing the room, although she never even made an attempt for the door.

She hit the far side of the tiny room. Her head jerked up and she snatched a teddy bear he hadn't noticed off the top of a book shelf tucked into the corner.

Crossing the room, she slammed it against his chest.

"What are you doing?" he asked, holding his hands back and refusing to take whatever she was trying to give him. Did she have another stash of drugs in there?

"After the break-in I called a friend who's a PI. He gave me several hidden cameras to place around the bar. There's one in that teddy bear. Take it. Watch it. I have no idea who's doing this, but it isn't me."

Finn stared at her, a sick mixture of emotions churning through his belly—hope, fear, disappointment. It scared him how much he wanted her words to be true. Was he deluding himself?

Maybe, but either way it was worth a few minutes of his time.

Nodding, he clutched the bear in his fist.

A few minutes later, Dade and Simmons walked into the office, grim expressions on both their faces.

Finn simply pointed to the open safe. Dade crossed the room, placed a hand on Tucker's shoulder and turned her. Grasping both of her wrists, the metallic click of cuffs closing around them echoed loudly through the room.

"Kentucky Blackburn, you're under arrest for possession with the intent to sell." He continued to read her the Miranda rights and when he asked her if she understood them her only comment was, "You're making a big mistake."

"That's what they all say," Simmons murmured, clearly unhappy with this turn of events.

Shaking her head, Tucker stared at him for several seconds, her gaze in complete turmoil...and then it just blanked out. And the woman he'd first met stood in front of him again. The detached owner of the bar. The woman who never let anyone in because everyone either left or failed her.

And that hurt almost more than realizing she wasn't the woman he'd thought.

Without another word, Dade and Simmons led Tucker from the room. The bar was silent as they walked her through the place. Finn trailed silently behind them, taking in the phones pointed in her direction, no doubt taking videos and pictures, posting to every social media site.

The fact that the owner of the Kentucky Rose had been arrested and led out in handcuffs would be all over town before Dade and Simmons even got her booked at the station.

Shit. Finn's belly writhed unhappily.

The door to the bar banged shut and sound erupted inside. Monique charged across the bar toward him. "What the hell happened?"

"She's been arrested for dealing meth."

Monique's mouth dropped open in complete shock before snapping shut. "If you believe that then you don't know her at all. Tucker would never do anything to jeopardize the Rose. God," her eyes screwed shut, "this is going to ruin her business."

A few days ago, Finn would have argued the same thing. The Tucker he knew wouldn't have ever done anything to hurt her bar. This place was her life. But if the bar was in trouble…? Wyatt's words rang through his ears one more time. If she was truly in financial trouble would she have grasped at straws and turned to something that would earn her quick money?

Wyatt joined them. Before he could ask, Monique gave him the run-down.

"What do you mean? How do you know she's been dealing? That doesn't sound like her at all."

Finn shook his head. "I found meth in her safe, guys. A lot of it. And there's evidence beyond that. It looks bad."

"You're wrong," Wyatt said, absolute certainty ringing in his voice.

God, he wanted his faith to be as rock solid, but it just wasn't possible. Not with all of the evidence mounted against her.

But the doubt was there. The look of devastation on Tucker's face…that was hard to fake.

A vision of that teddy bear, where he'd dropped it onto her desk as Dade and Simmons came in, filled his head.

He strode back into her office, desperation and hope tangling together as he snatched the bear up.

14

THE WALK TO that squad car was interminable. The expressions on her employees' faces…those hurt. All the customers gaping at her, too.

This was going to be everywhere within minutes. Social media could be such a curse at times like these. And no matter what happened, the Rose would forever be tainted by this story. Everyone would assume her bar was a seedy place and she'd lose customers.

The image she'd worked so hard to build had been damaged beyond repair.

But she couldn't worry about that right now. She had bigger things to deal with.

Finn's reaction made one thing clear, she was alone in this. Although, hadn't she always been?

For a few days he'd convinced her to forget the lessons she'd learned the hard way—that you could only depend on yourself.

Standing there, staring at him, as Dade had snapped those cuffs around her wrists, his cold expression had cut deep. Deeper than she could bear. Her chest literally ached, as if someone had taken their fist and punched it through her solar plexus.

That moment was her worst nightmare come to fruition. This, this was exactly what she'd spent her entire life avoiding.

Damn Finn for making her care—for making her trust him—and then walking away when she'd needed him to believe in her most.

The process of being booked was humiliating. They took mug shots and fingerprints. Her attorney showed up. Monique must have called him since Tucker hadn't had the chance. He specialized in business, but brought a friend of his who handled criminal cases.

She explained the entire situation to them.

"I really wish you'd waited to tell them about that camera, Tucker," Mark grumbled as he made notes on the yellow legal pad in front of him. "You're assuming they'll look at the footage and do the right thing if it exonerates you."

On that she had little doubt. Finn's sense of honor and inflexible view of right and wrong were the reason she was in this place. She had no doubt that if he watched it, and there was something on it that helped, he'd make damn sure everyone knew.

Although, Tucker wasn't sure it would matter. Even if they let her walk out of the station right now, the damage was done—not just to her business, but her relationship with Finn.

Eventually, both men left and an officer escorted her to a cell. Her chest tightened as the bars clanged shut behind her.

The space was stark and small, painted a depressing

shade of green-brown. There was a single bed, toilet and sink. At least she had the cell to herself.

It was late and, after everything that had happened, her body was exhausted. Curling up on the bed, Tucker was asleep within minutes, grateful for any respite from what she was dealing with.

What felt like only moments later, but was probably closer to several hours, the bars rumbled open again.

Simmons stood on the other side, the expression on his face even grimmer than it had been when he'd walked into her office to arrest her.

This wasn't going to be good.

Sweeping his arm out, he indicated she could leave the cell. Instead of leading her back down the hallway to one of the interrogation rooms, he took her to the women's bathroom, handed her the clothes and belongings she'd been wearing and said, "Get changed. I'll drive you home."

"Excuse me?"

"The tape is dark, so we can't identify the person who placed the drugs in your safe."

Then why the hell was he letting her go?

"But it's clear that whoever it is, isn't you…you're too damn small. In fact, we've been looking for a woman because that's what our informant told us. But it's clearly a man who accessed your safe. Any idea who that could be?"

Tucker closed her eyes. There were a few options, but she wasn't about to throw someone else under the bus. She'd just gotten herself out from under it.

"I've not shared the combination with anyone, but obviously that hasn't stopped someone. So I can't say for sure." She gave him a hard glance. "And I'm not certain I would if I could, considering I spent last night in jail despite the fact that I'm innocent."

Simmons sucked in a deep breath and let it out on a slow sigh. "I'm really sorry, Tucker."

Yeah, she'd just bet. "Little good that's going to do my business. My reputation—and the reputation of my bar—is ruined."

"I'll do whatever I can to help with that."

"Sure, because everyone pays attention when the police issue a mea culpa. No doubt *that* social media post won't go viral, unlike the pictures of me being led out in handcuffs."

He swore under his breath.

"My thought exactly."

"I suppose we've lost your cooperation in catching the real dealer?"

There was a part of her that wanted to tell him he could never darken her door again, but that would be stupid. This asshole, whoever it was, was just as responsible for ruining her business as Finn, Dade and Simmons were. More, since they'd just been doing their jobs.

"Of course not. I want this prick caught just as much as you do."

He nodded, waited outside the restroom as she changed then escorted her out to his car.

What hurt almost more than anything was that Finn wasn't the one doing this. Obviously, he'd seen the video and knew he was wrong. But he hadn't shown up to apologize and make it right.

Instead, he'd let Simmons handle the whole thing.

Just as well, because she had no idea what she wanted

to say to him when she saw him again. Whatever it was, wouldn't be nice.

Maybe it was better this way. Better if they never saw each other again.

It'd been late morning when Simmons had released her. Monique and Wyatt had both tried to convince her to take the night off, but she'd needed work—needed the Rose—so she'd come in. Now she was desperately trying to just get through the rest of the night. Obviously she was failing miserably at pretending everything was okay. Several of her waitresses had approached her, asking if there was anything they could do to help.

She'd explained to everyone that it had been a huge misunderstanding and she'd been released after all charges against her had been dropped.

But that didn't stop everyone from staring at her with concern and pity. Hopefully that would stop soon, because it was driving her crazy. She was used to being the one offering help, not the other way around. The whole situation made her uncomfortable.

The first several times, she'd told whoever asked that she was fine. But the more she said it, the more she realized it wasn't true. Not even close.

And she needed an outlet. The pain, anger and grief were just building inside her chest, expanding to the point of choking her. So when Monique came up to her after closing and asked her again if she was okay the truth just spilled out.

"No, I'm not. Everything is messed up."

Pulling her over to the bar, Monique poured her a shot of tequila and pushed it into her hand. "Do you mean the bar or Finn?"

The answer should be simple. The Rose should have been the only thing she really cared about, but the damage that'd been done didn't even rank compared to the seeping wound across her heart.

"Both." It was the honest answer. "But I'm not sure the Rose will recover. You saw the crowd tonight, not nearly as big as usual. The damage has already been done."

Grabbing another glass, Monique poured herself a shot, downed it, then took another.

"Whoa." Wasn't Tucker supposed to be the one drowning her misery?

Monique turned to her and for the first time, Tucker realized her eyes were glittering with tears. "I'm so sorry."

"About what?" Monique had nothing to apologize for. Please, let Monique's tears be sympathy and not what Tucker was seriously afraid of.

"I got into trouble a couple years ago. It started out as recreation—pot, pills, just on the weekends and at parties. For a good time, you know? But it quickly got out of hand. The guy I usually bought from was out one night and I *needed* a fix. So I contacted a friend who put me in touch with someone else. Long story short, I got busted."

"Oh, Monique." Tears welled in Tucker's eyes. How had she not known her friend was using? Had she been that blind and wrapped up in her own life? Or had Monique kept that to herself because she knew Tucker wouldn't approve?

Monique shook her head. "No. I don't need or deserve your pity. I did this to myself. A day or two after I was arrested, I received a phone call. This guy, voice disguised with one of those machines, told me if I agreed to work for him—for free—he could have the charges dropped. I mean, it was either face jail time, lose my entire life, including my husband, or agree to sell. I got help and got clean, but I couldn't shake this guy."

She dropped her head into her hands, rubbing across her face and spreading the silent tears. "I've tried, believe me. It's not all the time, but a couple times a week he sends people my way. Mostly airmen looking for a good time. Best I can figure, he chose me because of my job. It started when we were at that place downtown and followed me here. I'm so damn sorry, Tucker. You have no idea how much."

"I found some drugs last Friday night. Were those yours?"

"Yes. I don't like to keep them on me during shift."

"What about the meth in my safe? Was that you too?" Tucker wasn't sure she really wanted to know the answer. How would she feel if one of her best friends had set her up? But she needed to know.

"No!" Monique leaned forward, her gaze earnest and imploring. "I have no idea who put them there, Tucker. I swear. If I did I'd tell you."

Okay, this was bad. But it could be worse. She believed Monique when her friend told her she was clean. She had a family who depended on her.

But maybe this was the break they'd all been waiting for. Maybe they could catch the person responsible for this entire mess and extricate Monique at the same time.

"You need to tell Finn what you know."

"Why would I do that?"

"Because he's working on a joint task force with the police."

"I knew there was more to him than met the eye! I

mean, aside from the way he watched you like he was afraid you might disappear."

Tucker scoffed. "Yeah, right."

"No, really. That man is head over heels for you, Tucker. And you're blind if you don't see it."

"He had me arrested, Monique."

"Because obviously someone wanted him to."

"And he wasn't there when they released me and hasn't shown up since then. You're wrong. You didn't see the look on his face when he found that meth in my safe. The cops might have let me go, but he clearly still thinks I'm guilty. And I'm not sure I can trust someone who obviously doesn't trust me."

Tucker shook her head. Saying the words out loud hurt even more than thinking them. Reaching for the bottle, she poured herself another shot and downed it. No, that wouldn't fix the problem, but right now she'd take any help at dulling the sharp edge of pain.

"It doesn't matter. The only thing that does is fixing this whole mess. You know who's behind all of this. You can stop it, Monique."

"I don't," she said. "That's the problem. If I could've turned him in I would have done it a long time ago. I've actually never met the guy. He calls me, disguising his voice every time, and the number he uses is always disconnected when I try to call back. The few times I've refused to do what he's asked he's sent photos not only from my first bust, but of me selling since then. He's got me tied up in a neat little bow and I know next to nothing. I have to assume I'm not the only person he's blackmailing. If you think about it, it's the perfect set-up. I don't have anything to use against him, while he has my entire life teetering on the edge of disaster. And

I don't even get a cut of the sales—not that I'd take dirty money anyway."

"Crap!" Frustration rode Tucker hard. "I don't think that matters anymore, Monique. You need to go to the police and tell them what you do know. Maybe they can add it to the other pieces they already have and come up with the answer. This whole thing is going to collapse eventually and you want to be on the right side when it does."

"I know."

"I'm here for you." Tucker reached over and pulled Monique into a hug. "You've made some mistakes, but no one deserves to pay for them indefinitely. Whatever you need, I'll help."

Monique's arms went around her waist, squeezing tight. Pulling back, she tried to hide a sniffle, but couldn't wish away the tears. "I don't deserve you. Not after bringing this to your front door."

Tucker shook her head. Maybe a month ago, or even yesterday, her reaction would have been different. But after spending the night in jail, she realized that sometimes bad things happened and the difference between those who lost everything and those who came out of the dark determined to survive was the people standing beside them.

She didn't have many she could count on, but Monique was on the short list. And, unlike Finn, she had no intention of abandoning her friend when she needed her most.

"Come on," Monique said. "I'll help you close up." While they'd been talking, the rest of the staff had headed out. "It's too late to do anything tonight. I'll

talk with Michael when I get home and contact the authorities in the morning."

"Let me know when. I know a couple good cops and
a great lawyer. I'll call them. Go with you."

In companionable silence, the two of them puttered
around the bar, taking care of the last-minute details
necessary to close up and prepare for tomorrow.

It felt weird walking out to the parking lot without
Finn and Duchess beside her. Waving at Monique across
the lot, Tucker got into her car and headed home. A
few blocks away, sitting at a stoplight, she reached for
her phone. Not that she expected to see a missed call
or text from Finn…but she couldn't quite stop herself
from looking. It had been a compulsion all night, one
she'd finally solved by shoving her phone into a drawer
behind the bar.

Which was exactly where it still was.

Groaning, Tucker made a U-turn when the light
turned green and headed back to the Rose. Parking in
the back lot, she snatched her keys from the ignition,
raced for the door and dashed inside. She didn't even
bother flipping on lights, just headed straight for the
bar. Less than two minutes and she planned to be on
her way out again.

Until she barreled straight into Dade.

"Oomph," she said, her hands flattening against his
chest to insulate her from the impact. "What are you
doing here?"

Wait.

"How'd you get in?"

His hands wrapped around her arms, holding her in
place when she tried to pull away.

Until that moment, she hadn't been scared. Maybe

she should have been, but her brain had processed who was standing in her bar before she'd smacked into him. And her instinct said he was fine.

But now…the way he was holding her had uneasiness flipping through her belly.

"Are there other cameras, Tucker?"

She shook her head, trying to switch mental gears and focus on what he was asking.

"What?"

"That hidden camera was clever. It never occurred to me you'd seek outside help. I just assumed, thanks to your budding relationship with the good soldier, that you'd turn to him. And he'd tell me everything. Well, everything except fucking you. That little detail he kept to himself."

And, yet, he still obviously knew their relationship had taken that turn. The unease skating across Tucker's skin ramped up to full-fledged panic.

Nope, she couldn't give in. This was not the time to lose her head.

"You're damn lucky the lighting sucked and no one could tell it was me."

"*I'm* the lucky one?" The snide comment was out of her mouth before she'd even thought it through. Fury flashed through Dade's eyes and his fingers dug painfully into her arms. She was going to have bruises in the morning…if she made it out of this alive.

"You're the one who planted the drugs in my safe. How?"

"Safes are a hobby of mine. And you really need to hire better staff. No one even noticed when I slipped down the back hallway through the door they like to leave open."

Spinning her, Dade wrenched her arms behind her back. "But enough chitchat. I'm going to ask you again. Any more hidden cameras around this place? Any other devices that might implicate me in this mess?"

Craning her head sideways, Tucker ignored the pull on her shoulders and glared at Dade. "You're the one blackmailing Monique."

"McAllister wasn't wrong. You're a smart one."

"Why are you doing this?" Although she could probably answer that question for herself, she wanted to hear him say it.

"Money. Believe it or not, I started out brimming with ideals. But it didn't take long for that to change. I watched hardened criminals, people guilty of the worst crimes, walk free over and over, and there was nothing I could do about it."

"So you decided to join them? Yeah, great strategy."

She didn't see the blow coming. The punch landed just below her ribs and sent her lurching forward. The only thing that kept her from sprawling onto the floor was his hold on her arm.

Her breath wheezed out, but she wasn't about to stop now. "So, what? You have the power to make their charges disappear, then you blackmail them into working for you and keep all the money for yourself. The more laws they break, the tighter your noose around their necks."

Dade's hold on her arms tightened to the point where she couldn't stay upright. With a whimper, she doubled over to relieve the pressure in her shoulders. "You're despicable. Worse than anyone you might have caught."

"It doesn't matter. I always knew it would end at some point. I've got enough money stashed away to live comfortably. For years I managed to lead any investigation into my activities in the other direction. But now, that's becoming impossible to continue. I needed someone to take the fall."

"Me."

He shrugged. Tucker could feel the motion as his chest rose and fell against her back. "I didn't plan to frame you, but you made it so damn easy. Your fingerprints on those drugs and then withholding your surveillance footage."

Bastard.

"With everyone busy congratulating themselves on capturing the bad guy, I decided to quietly go out on a win and retire."

And she'd put a crimp in his plans, thanks to that teddy bear with the hidden camera.

"Finn mentioned you told him there were more cameras when you informed him about the first one. So, tell me where they are."

"Not a chance." There was no way in hell she was going to let this asshole get away with this. Not only had he attempted to ruin her life and her business, he'd ruined countless other lives—including Monique's. He'd taken advantage of people who needed help.

"Don't test me, Tucker. Do you know I've been trained in interrogation tactics? And not just the sanctioned ones."

Fear skittered down her spine, but she refused to bend or relent.

"You are stubborn, aren't you?" Using his hold on her, Dade frog-marched her out into the center of the dark, empty bar.

The place was quiet and peaceful, the way she normally liked it best. But not now.

Twisting her around, he didn't give her time to duck before another punch landed just beneath her jaw, snapping her head backward. A third landed in her exposed belly, knocking the wind right out of her. The next had her sprawling on the floor, the room swimming around her.

"Tell me where they are, Tucker, and this can end right now."

She tried to scramble away. To use the tables and chairs as barriers, but he didn't give her the chance. Instead, Dade sent the toe of his heavy boot straight into her ribs. Merciless. Sadistic.

Instinct had her curling up into a ball, protecting her belly and head as best she could. But she couldn't stay that way indefinitely. There was no way she was making it out of this. No way he would let her survive. She knew too much. The minute she told him what he wanted she was as good as dead.

No, that wasn't how this was going to end.

Tucker used every last ounce of strength she possessed in a burst that had her surging up from the floor, racing for the front door.

She made it several steps, but no more. His hand tangled in her hair, jerking her backwards. Tears of pain welled in her eyes, but that didn't stop her from grasping her own hair and jerking in the opposite direction, hoping to break his hold.

It didn't work. Instead, he used her momentum to swing her around and smash her into a nearby table.

A groan wheezed out of her suddenly useless lungs. Her body collapsed, rolling off the table and slamming into the floor.

Then he started kicking again.

"Such a shame," he said, watching her feeble attempt to crawl away. The passive, calm expression on his face, even as he delivered another vicious kick, made her skin crawl. "Everyone will be devastated when this place burns to the ground, the owner's body found charred inside."

Dade crouched down beside her, picking up a strand of her blond hair and running his fingers down it. "There's more than one way to make sure no one finds those hidden cameras, Tucker."

She saw it coming, but couldn't do anything to stop it. The punch landed right upside her temple. Everything around her went fuzzy and then finally black.

15

GODDAMMIT. FINN STARED at the screen, a sick sensation rolling through his gut.

This wasn't the first time he'd watched the video. Apparently, he couldn't stop torturing himself with it.

Staring at the footage in front of him, a man furtively glanced around Tucker's office before pulling out a set of tools that he used to crack the code on the safe. Then he stuffed it with the drugs and money.

The first time he'd watched, he'd been elated to realize Tucker was as innocent as she'd said. Until he realized that meant he hadn't believed her when she'd needed him—begged him—to stand beside her.

The second time, he'd just stared at the footage, silently condemning himself.

Now, the fifth time, he was finally paying attention to the little details he'd missed the first few times through. And while it was dark, which made it difficult to identify the person by their facial features, he was picking up on other things.

And, maybe, if he hadn't spent the last several weeks working with the man he wouldn't have noticed the tiny curl of ink that flashed over the collar of his shirt, but he had. And he knew the tattoo because he'd asked Dade about it the first time they'd met.

Goddammitalltohell. It actually explained a lot. From the very beginning he'd thought there was an inside man. He'd just assumed *inside* meant the Rose, not the damn task force.

For a brief second, he thought about calling in Simmons. But considering how close the partners were, he couldn't discount the idea they were in this together.

He'd been played. The events of the night Tucker had been arrested rolled through his mind. Dade's subtle suggestion he was missing something, which had prompted him to take Duchess into Tucker's office in the first place.

She'd been purposely set up—by a man who was supposed to be one of the good guys.

Grabbing his cell, he called Tucker. He had to warn her. Now that the charges against her had been dropped there was no telling what Dade might do. But her cell rang several time before going to voicemail. Was she screening him or asleep? It was late, even for her.

Grabbing his keys, he hollered for Duchess and raced out to his Jeep. He held the door open, and she jumped inside. He'd swing by the Rose first, since it was on the way to her house. He'd decide his next steps once he could pin her down.

The drive to the bar felt like it took forever. The night was quiet, which only made everything worse. His brain spun, replaying over and over again the expression on Tucker's face as he watched Dade clamp those cuffs around her wrists.

The devastation. The betrayal. The complete and

utter defeat. She'd placed her trust in him, something he knew was difficult for her. No, he'd forced her to place her trust in him. He'd given her no choice in the matter, smashing through every roadblock she'd placed in his path because he'd wanted her and that was all that mattered at the time.

But that wasn't the case anymore.

Her pain had hurt him—then and now. Even when he'd thought she was guilty—a drug dealer—he'd cared about her. He'd wanted to save her, even if he needed to save her from herself.

Shit, he'd screwed up royally. Forcing her to trust him but not giving her the same in return. Not believing her when she'd said she was innocent, anger and brimstone firing from those deep blue eyes.

He was so lost in thought that he didn't notice the smoke curling up from the building until he careened into the empty parking lot. And then all he could think was that Tucker just couldn't catch a damn break.

Her car wasn't in the front lot, but it wouldn't be if she was home. Phone already to his ear, 911 on the line to report the fire, Finn barreled around the building to the back.

And his heart sank into his shoes when he saw her car parked right beside the back door.

God, Tucker was inside.

Not even bothering to turn off the Jeep, Finn burst out, letting the door swing wide. He raced for the back entrance only to find it locked.

Of course it was. The security lock engaged from the inside.

The urge to pound helplessly on the door was overwhelming, but that wouldn't accomplish anything.

Tucker needed him, so he needed to keep a calm head. He'd never forgive himself if she died inside while he stood by helplessly, unable to do anything.

The sensation, so like what he'd felt staring down at his sister's lifeless body, nearly sent him to his knees.

Racing back to the Jeep, Finn riffled around the tool-box he kept behind the back seat until he found the small hatchet.

He attacked the door, never so thankful that Tucker had that authentic heavy wooden door, even in the back. It took several swings, but eventually the thing splintered. Reaching into the gap, Finn pulled the door from the hinges, letting it clatter to the ground.

Heat and smoke rolled out, nearly choking him and sending him straight to his knees, gasping for clean air.

Beside him, Duchess whined. She nosed against him, barked and then stared inside the dark building. How the hell was he going to find her in this huge place?

Duchess whined again and took a tentative step forward, looking back at him for instructions.

Holding her head in his hands, Finn looked straight into Duchess' deep brown eyes and said, "Find her, girl. Please. I need you to lead me to her."

TUCKER COUGHED. HER EYES popped open only to realize she still couldn't see.

Her entire body ached and her eyes burned. Smoke, thick and dirty gray, swirled around her, stealing her breath.

Fire. The Rose was on fire.

Palms to the floor, Tucker pushed up onto her knees, biting back a whimper of pain. Everything hurt, but that didn't matter right now. She needed to find a way out.

Was she still in the middle of the bar? Which way had she fallen? Which way was the door?

Panic paralyzed her for several seconds. She was so afraid of making the wrong move and finding herself in even more trouble.

But inaction meant dying in the middle of her bar, and Tucker was damned determined that wasn't going to happen. If she died here, Dade won and would get away with everything he'd done.

Twisting around, she tried to figure out which direction felt hottest. Her plan was to go the opposite way, figuring away from the flames was the best choice. If she could run into a wall or the bar she could orient herself and find her way out.

Every joint in her body throbbed, but she continued to crawl forward, yelping each time she ran into a table or chair along the way.

How long had she been unconscious? There was no way to know. Long enough for the bar to fill up with smoke. She needed to get out so she could call for help, although her cell was still in the drawer behind the bar.

Her body heaved on a racking cough. Her lungs burned and her ribs ached. It felt like she was dragging air three inches thick through the smallest spaces of her body as she breathed. And the heat. It was everywhere. Her clothes felt like they were melting onto her skin.

But she didn't have time to stop. Any inch forward was better than certain death.

Her head started swimming again, the room going wonky. The floor felt like it was tilting beneath her.

No. She couldn't black out again. Not if she wanted to live, and she did. Her life might be completely screwed up right now, but it was hers and she wanted it.

Wanted Finn.

Shit. Wanted his annoying antics and his arrogant attitude. The sweetness he kept to himself more often than he should. The brilliant way he observed the world, seeing it just the way it was. She wanted his strength and his ability to make her feel strong even as he managed to care for her—especially when she made it difficult.

She wanted his love. She wanted his trust.

She wanted something she could never have.

Tucker had no idea if the tears tracking down her face were from the smoke or the overwhelming grief sweeping through her. It didn't matter. The emotions were enough to push her when every muscle in her body was screaming that she'd had enough.

But even then, she was afraid she wasn't going to make it. The smoke was getting thicker and she still had no idea where she was—or how close the exit might be.

Her body felt like it weighed three tons, each limb getting heavier and heavier when she'd pick it up to crawl forward.

Nope, she wasn't willing to give up. If she died tonight, she was going to do it fighting.

Suddenly, a sound echoed through the darkness. Startling because it was out of place among the crackle and hiss of the fire.

The clank of metal tags and the scrabble of nails across the wooden floor.

"Duchess?" Tucker croaked, the sound practically nonexistent. She was almost too afraid to hope. Maybe she was hallucinating. Her brain conjuring up the one sound she associated with Finn because wherever he went Duchess was never far behind.

The swirl of smoke in front of her cleared and the

most amazing sight greeted her. Not a mirage. Duchess charged forward, letting out several loud barks.

Tucker collapsed, her body simply giving out and the tears started streaming faster.

Wrapping her arms around Duchess's neck, Tucker buried her face in the soft fur. "I've never been so happy to see you in my life," she whispered.

"Tucker?" Finn's voice echoed through the bar.

"Here. We're here," she screamed, or what was meant to be a scream, but was more like a raspy whimper. Beside her, Duchess barked again, loud and long.

Finn charged out of the smoke, a warrior hell-bent on conquering something, even if it was just a few flames.

"Good girl," he said, patting Duchess on the head even as he leaned down and scooped Tucker up into his arms.

A wet T-shirt fell against her belly. "Put that over your mouth and nose."

Looking down at the dog sitting beside them, he said, "Get us out of here," and then followed close behind as Duchess moved through the bar.

It felt like forever, but it was probably no more than a minute before they broke through the back door into blessed, clean air.

Tucker pulled in a huge gulp of it, nearly passing out again when her lungs couldn't take it and she started hacking and wheezing.

Finn didn't stop until they were on the far side of the back parking lot. Gently setting her onto the grass, he leaned back and took stock of her.

God, she had to look a mess. Bloody, bruised, soot covered and filthy. But thanks to him and Duchess, alive.

"Thank you," she managed between fits of coughing. "Dade. He's the one who's been selling drugs. Set the bar on fire. I can't prove it."

Not without the cameras that were no doubt already melted and useless.

"I know, but don't worry about that right now. Just lie still. Paramedics and fire are on their way."

"You know?"

Finn nodded. "That was the reason I came looking for you. But even if I didn't already know, I'd believe you. I promise I'll never doubt you again."

In the distance, Tucker caught the first hint of sirens.

Giving in to the exhaustion overwhelming her, she collapsed backward, her eyes squeezing shut.

There was nothing left for her to do but wait and see how bad the damage was when the smoke cleared.

JESUS, HE WANTED to bombard her with questions. Why did she look like she'd gone ten rounds with a heavyweight champion and lost? Was there any way on this earth she'd ever forgive him? Ever place her trust in him again?

But now wasn't the time for any of that.

His hands were shaking, something he hadn't realized until he leaned forward to brush some hair away from Tucker's temple.

God, he could have lost her tonight. That realization would have sent him to his knees if he wasn't already there, beside her on the grass.

He watched her whole body convulse with another round of coughing, and he grumbled unkind words beneath his breath. The paramedics needed to get here three minutes ago.

The helpless sensation was driving him crazy.

He heard the first fire truck pull up on the other side of the building. He wasn't about to wait for them to realize someone was around back. Scooping Tucker into his arms again, he tried to ignore her whimper and the way her entire body shuddered from pain. He headed around to the front just as an ambulance and another engine arrived.

The minute they saw him, the paramedics charged in his direction. "She needs oxygen. And she's got other injuries. I'm not sure how or why, but it looks like she's been beaten."

One of the EMTs produced an oxygen mask and fit it over Tucker's face. A firefighter rushed up to him, "Anyone else inside?"

"Not that I know of. Tucker?"

Her eyes opened for the first time since they'd made it out of the building. It hurt to see them dulled by pain and grief that he knew he was partly responsible for putting there.

She reached up to move the mask, but the EMT stopped her, so she just shook her head.

One of the hardest things Finn had ever done was to stand back and watch the professionals take care of her. His heart was pounding inside his chest, a combination of adrenaline and fear. They rushed, but in his head it wasn't nearly fast enough.

He stood there, helpless, hands clasped to the top of his head. Until Tucker's hand moved from the gurney they'd placed her on, motioning him closer.

He took a step, and then another, until he was standing beside her. She reached for him, grasped his hand and squeezed.

Looking down at her, face a blotchy mess, soot covering everything, he realized she'd never looked more beautiful. Because she was here, alive and silently asking for him.

Dropping his head down to her shoulder, Finn whispered, "I don't know what I'd do if anything happened to you, Tucker. It hurt so much to lose my sister. I blamed myself for years. Losing you would be just as devastating. I don't think I could survive that kind of pain twice."

Her fingers tangled in his hair, gripping hard and pulling him back so she could look at him. With the other, she reached up and pulled the mask away, batting at the hand that tried to stop her.

"Apparently, I'm damn hard to kill," she rasped. "Although Dade sure as hell tried. Tell Simmons to meet us at the hospital, I have quite a bit of information to tell him about his partner." The grim expression on Tucker's face made Finn's heart squeeze.

"There'll be plenty of time for that, Tucker. Right now, we need to get you checked out."

"No. I want him, Finn. He burned down my bar."

Of course she did.

"You don't think Simmons could be involved?"

"No. I'm certain Dade was working alone."

"All right. I'll have Simmons meet us, but you're not talking to anyone until the doctor clears you."

She grumbled. The EMT reached out and placed the mask over her face again. It didn't quite hide the glare she was giving him, not that it would do her much good. On this, he wasn't budging. Her health was a hell of a lot more important than anything else at this moment, and he'd do whatever it took to make sure she was okay.

Even if that meant protecting her from herself.

She gave his hand one more squeeze before they loaded her into the ambulance and, sirens blaring, raced out of the parking lot.

Finn was at the Jeep seconds later, calling Duchess who hopped inside right away. The red-orange glow of flames licked against the inky sky behind him. It hurt to see the Rose in that condition, because he knew how much it would hurt Tucker.

But they'd make it right. Whatever it took, he'd help her rebuild.

16

THE NEXT AFTERNOON, Tucker was resting in her hospital bed. With all of her injuries, they'd wanted to keep her at least a day, so she was stuck for now.

Plus, there was no way Finn was going to let her leave, even if she was chomping at the bit to get her first look at the Rose.

She didn't trust he was telling her the truth when he said the damage wasn't that bad. Besides, she had no idea how he'd know, considering he hadn't left the hospital since he'd arrived.

"If you pace across this floor one more time, I'm going to have to hurt you," she murmured, trying her best to keep her jaw from moving too much.

Her entire body ached. She had a couple of cracked ribs, lots of minor cuts and a rainbow of bruises.

Finn shot her a grim look, but dropped into the chair beside the bed. So far, he hadn't said much. At one point she'd tried to start a conversation with him, but he'd basically shut her down and told her they'd talk when she felt better.

Maybe that was smarter, considering the pain meds

they'd given her. They were making her feel pretty floaty.

She couldn't stop watching him. Not just the fluid motion of his body as he'd paced around her room, but his agitation and restlessness. He'd been that way from the moment they'd wheeled her in.

It didn't take a genius to figure out he wanted to smash something. For her. But was holding back because he knew she needed him.

If she'd had any second thoughts about this man, they fled as she watched him. Yes, he was career military, but that didn't matter anymore. Not when the heart of him was so beautiful and pure. She'd deal with whatever came with loving him, because no matter how hard she'd tried, she couldn't stop.

Finn's cell rang. He glanced at it, grimaced, then answered, "McAllister."

He grunted a couple of times, said, "Yeah, I'll take care of it," and then hung up.

Reaching beside her, he grabbed the controls attached to the bed and turned the TV on. Flipping through, he stopped at one of the news stations. A picture of Simmons filled the screen…standing in front of her bar.

Okay. So, from the little she could see, at least it hadn't burned to the ground. The roof clearly had some damage, but the rest…

Maybe Finn wasn't lying to her.

"I'm happy to report that after months of work, a joint drug task force has apprehended a high-priority meth dealer whose product has been linked to several accidental deaths in recent months."

It didn't escape her that Simmons left out one tiny detail—the man had been a member of the police force.

No doubt, they were hoping to keep that piece of information under wraps for as long as possible.

Simmons had met them both at the hospital, and her statement had been enough for him to call in Internal Affairs. Things had unfolded rather quickly over the last twenty-four hours. Now that they had information pointing them in the right direction, they were able to find overseas accounts in Dade's name, holding millions of dollars in illicit funds.

After leaving Tucker for dead, Dade had attempted to flee the country, but was stopped by Border Patrol on his way into Mexico.

"Why is he standing in front of my damn bar issuing this statement?" Holy hell. With the obvious fire damage, he made it look like the Rose was the location of the bust.

Pushing up from the bed, Tucker swung her legs over the side. One hand gripped the line running fluids and drugs into her arm. She wanted to yank the thing out, walk out of this place, find Simmons and hurt him.

Finn's hand landed heavily over hers. The other grasped her ankles and swung her legs back into the bed. "Keep watching."

"When Ms. Blackburn was informed that someone was selling drugs inside her bar, she immediately agreed to cooperate with the authorities. Her arrest earlier this week was an effort to flush out the actual guilty parties."

She collapsed back onto the hard bed. "Well, well, well. Who knew Simmons was such a smooth liar?"

Finn shrugged. "It was hardly intentional, but that's what happened, isn't it? Me having you arrested put you in danger, Tucker. Made you a target."

His mouth thinned, his eyes narrowing into unhappy slits.

"You had no way of knowing that would happen."

"Maybe not, but I should have listened. Believed you."

"Yeah, you should have." What else was she supposed to say? That was the truth. And it would be a long time before the hurt of that went away completely. But, honestly, it was already starting to fade.

"But with the drugs in your safe and what Wyatt had told me…"

She was so damn tired of thinking about those drugs in her safe. Wait. "What did Wyatt tell you?"

"That you'd had some financial trouble when your refrigerator leaked and were up to your eyeballs in debt."

Tucker groaned and then grasped her ribs when the sound sent a wave of pain shooting through her. "That idiot. I was upset at the damage, obviously, but more so because I'd been saving to make some improvements to the bar and that disaster made me dip into what I had. It was an emotional blow more than a financial one. The only debt I'm carrying is the mortgage for the bar and my house."

Grasping her hand, he squeezed. "Good to know."

Simmons's voice pulled her attention back to the TV. "Unfortunately, Ms. Blackburn's agreement to assist us placed her in harm's way. Early yesterday morning she was assaulted, her place of business the target of arson."

"By the way, they're adding the arson and attempted murder charges to the others for Dade."

"Beautiful." Maybe she should have felt vindicated, but instead she just felt sad.

The story on screen faded away to a commercial.

Finn flipped it off, tossing the remote to the end of the bed.

Turning, he set his hip at the edge of her bed and grasped both of her hands in his. For several seconds he stared down at where they were joined.

Tucker watched him. Really watched him. And saw every emotion that flitted across his face, before it finally settled on guilt.

Looking up, he simply said, "I'm sorry."

The words were so stark and clearly heartfelt. They encompassed so much. And, yet, she still needed more. "For?"

"Everything? For not trusting in you when I'd done everything to crack through your protective layers and force you to trust me. For unwittingly putting you in a position that placed you in danger. For not protecting you. For the pain I know you feel because someone you trusted betrayed you."

He squeezed both hands. "Promise me, no matter what you decide about us, you won't let this become a reason to build those walls even higher. You're an amazing woman, Tucker. You deserve to be happy. To be surrounded by people who love you no matter what. Who'll be there for you."

His words petered out and he simply sat there, drilling her with that same deep, observant expression that had snared her the first time they met. He saw so much, more than anyone else she'd ever known.

At first that had left her feeling uncomfortable. But now…it made her feel safe. Because she didn't have to hide or pretend with him.

And even though there were no guarantees, she knew with Finn McAllister she would always know exactly where she stood. He'd protect her and support her. He'd call her on her bullshit. He'd work beside her if she let him.

He'd give her everything. As long as she promised to do the same.

"What do you mean, whatever I decide about us?"

Hope swirled through his gaze. "Kentucky Rose." She huffed. He ignored her. "You stormed across that bar and into my life. In a few short days you've become the most important person in my world. I can't imagine a single day without you beside me. I want the chance to build something with you. To prove that you can place your faith in me. To show you that I'll earn your love."

A lump formed in the back of her throat. Tucker swallowed hard. "Silly man," she said, her voice scratchy. Darn smoke. Leaning forward, she placed her hands on either side of his face and drew him closer. "You ask that like I have a choice, when you know damn well you really didn't give me one. I won't deny there's a part of me screaming to push you away, to protect myself from getting hurt. But that would be silly because living without you in my life would hurt so much more."

"Tucker," he breathed, right before finding her mouth and kissing her deeply. She sank into it, letting his mouth and words soothe all the places that still ached.

Although she wasn't quite done. After several moments, she pushed him away. Reaching between them, she pinched his shoulder.

"Ouch! What the heck was that for?" he asked, rubbing the spot.

"Don't think that means you're not going to have to make all of this up to me. You owe me, and I intend to make you pay."

Finn chuckled, scooping her up off the bed and into his lap. "Oh, yeah? I'm sure we can negotiate," he said, right before kissing her again. This time, his hands started wandering beneath the flimsy gown they'd wrapped her in.

And somewhere beside them, her monitors started beeping faster and faster, not that either of them noticed.

* * * * *

Smokejumper Tate McKnight heats up
Sweetheart, South Carolina...
and the girl he left behind...
in Kira Sinclair's next sizzling
Blaze story:

UP IN FLAMES

In stores May 2017.

Luca didn't get back to his new place until just after 8:00 p.m. It had turned blustery, and he rubbed his cold hands together as he entered the elevator.

Finally. He had his own apartment. Tomorrow his king bed and wide-screen TV would be delivered.

Ten minutes later he thought he heard the buzzer, but no way was the pizza he ordered here that fast. A moment later a scream rang out.

He grabbed the crowbar sitting on a pile of rags, his heart racing. It occurred to him that the scream didn't sound like a "help, I'm being assaulted" scream.

He moved closer to the door. Another scream, this time louder. It was coming from inside his apartment.

Luca glanced up the stairs. Goddamn Wes Holland hadn't moved out. Or he had, but he'd left a woman behind.

Cursing, he started up the staircase. As he moved stealthily down the hallway he heard her shouting. "Bastard" came in the clearest, followed by a wail.

He waited at the edge of the door, finally able to hear her words.

"How the hell does promising to pay me back do me any good?"

The tears and desperation came through loud and clear.

"That was all my savings," she said. "I hate you. You're such a coward, you won't even pick up."

Luca assumed the woman was talking about Wes and leaving him a voice mail. Had he really run off with her money?

He risked peeking inside the room. Luckily, the woman had her back to him. Lucky for him because it was a very nice view: the woman was wearing nothing but underwear.

Very tiny underwear.

Her bikini panties were pale blue, resting high on each cheek, just far enough to make him catch his breath. On top, he spotted the straps of her matching bra poking out from underneath a cascade of thick auburn hair.

He wondered what she looked like from the front…

She turned quickly, probably hearing his irregular breathing.

Now her scream was definitely of the "help, I'm being assaulted" variety.

He lowered the crowbar, noticing the two large suitcases behind her. "Hey," he said softly. "I'm not going to hurt you."

She waved her cell phone at him as she grabbed the nearest thing at hand—a pillow—and held it up against her semi-naked body. "I've already hit my panic button. The police will be here any minute."

"Good," he said, leaning his weapon against the door frame, trying hard to ignore the fact that she was hot. Certainly way too hot for that douchebag, Wes. "I'm anxious to hear you explain what you're doing in my apartment."

"*Your* apartment? You mean you own the one below?"

He nodded. "It's all one unit."

"But I have a key. And five days left on the rental agreement."

"What agreement?"

"My…" Her pause was notable, mostly for the look of fury that passed across her face. "My jerkface former business partner rented this place from the— From you, I guess. But I didn't think you lived here."

"Huh. Well, I think you might have been misinformed by Jerkface. I'm assuming you mean Wes Holland?"

Her whole demeanor changed from fierce guardedness to utter defeat. "Wait a minute. How do I know you're the real owner?"

"I understand you must be angry," he said, "but that doesn't change the fact that you'll have to leave."

"What? *Now?*"

"Well, no." It was already late, and he couldn't see himself throwing her out. "First thing tomorrow."

Pick up DARING IN THE CITY by Jo Leigh,
available in January 2017 wherever you buy
Harlequin® Blaze® books.

www.Harlequin.com

Turn your love of reading into rewards you'll love with
Harlequin My Rewards